"Have you ever been married?"

"Have you?" he came back smoothly.

"Certainly not," she snapped.

"Why not?"

Danie frowned at his persistence. "Why haven't you?"

He shrugged broad shoulders. "Simple enough. I haven't found the right woman yet."

"The right woman?" she repeated dazedly.

"Of course," Jonas replied.

Danie stared at him. The right woman! Was he serious?

Jonas chuckled. "Don't look so horrified, Danie," he grinned. "I'm one of an old-fashioned breed, I'm afraid. One man, one woman. As long as—"

"She's the right one," Danie finished for him huskily.

Some women are *meant* to wed!

Meet the Summer sisters:
Harriet, Danielle and Andrea
(or Harrie, Danie and Andie to their friends!).
All three are beautiful, intelligent and successful,
but they've always found their careers more
satisfying than their love lives.... Until now!

None of the sisters are looking for love—
but then destiny causes Quinn, Jonas
and Adam to cross their paths.
Will these exceptional men pop the question?

Don't miss any of the
fabulous BACHELOR SISTERS stories
by popular Harlequin Presents® author
CAROLE MORTIMER!

Harrie's story:
To Have a Husband
July 2001

Danie's story:
To Become a Bride
August 2001

Andie's story:
To Make a Marriage
September 2001

Carole Mortimer

TO BECOME A BRIDE

BACHELOR
SISTERS

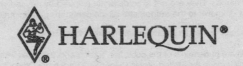

HARLEQUIN®

TORONTO • NEW YORK • LONDON
AMSTERDAM • PARIS • SYDNEY • HAMBURG
STOCKHOLM • ATHENS • TOKYO • MILAN • MADRID
PRAGUE • WARSAW • BUDAPEST • AUCKLAND

ISBN 0-373-12194-6

TO BECOME A BRIDE

First North American Publication 2001.

Copyright © 2001 by Carole Mortimer.

PROLOGUE

'MR NOBLE?'

He slowly opened one sleepy eyelid above an even sleepier, bloodshot eye. Only to raise the other eyelid, above an equally bloodshot eye, and find himself looking into the most amazing green eyes he had ever seen.

They weren't the green he usually associated with eye colour, that faded colour that could look a hazelly grey, but the deep, deep green of a clear-cut emerald. High cheekbones sided a pert nose, the skin was clear and smooth, the mouth had a mischievous quirk to it even though it was unsmiling at this moment, and the chin pointed and raised determinedly.

The rest of the woman was harder to distinguish, Jonas realised a little irritably. A black baseball cap was pulled low over those amazing green eyes, her hair tucked neatly inside it, although the lashes that surrounded her eyes were dark and long. Black combat trousers were worn beneath a black fleece top, the latter zipped up to her creamy throat.

Obviously a young woman who liked to be taken seriously, he noted with amusement.

'Is something funny?' the woman prompted sharply.

'Not at all,' Jonas drawled dismissively, swinging long legs from over the arm of his chair to the floor before straightening in his seat.

'Then I take it you are Mr Noble?' the woman repeated abruptly.

He looked around the luxurious but otherwise deserted private lounge before glancing back up at the young woman with mocking brown eyes. 'I would think that's a pretty sure bet,' he finally drawled caustically; he didn't suffer fools any more gladly than this young woman appeared to!

Anger flared briefly in those dark green eyes, but was quickly brought back under control. 'If you've finished your coffee—' she looked down pointedly at the empty cup on the table in front of him '—your flight is ready to leave any time.'

He wasn't sure he was going to be ready, in the full sense of the word, any time today. Despite the pint of strong coffee he had consumed since his arrival fifteen minutes ago! It had been a long night, involving no sleep, and flying off to God-knew-where, to meet a man he didn't even know, was not high on his list of priorities at this particular moment.

But he had agreed—under pressure!—to today's meeting yesterday when he'd received the telephone call from Jerome Summer, and he was a man of his word. So, despite the change of circumstances which meant he hadn't actually been to bed yet, he had duly presented himself at this private lounge situated within the much larger complex of the airport. But that didn't mean he had to like it!

He stood up, flexing tired muscles. 'That's some uniform you have there,' he murmured derisively. If he had expected to be pampered by a sexy flight attendant on this short, but, his host considered, necessary flight, then he was obviously in for a disappointment!

'Uniform?' the woman repeated abruptly, looking down frowningly at her dark clothing. 'These are my own clothes, Mr Noble,' she told him coldly.

Obviously Jerome Summer ran a relaxed ship, Jonas acknowledged. It was none of his business how the other man dealt with his staff, but Jonas's own experience had taught him that familiarity bred contempt; become too relaxed with someone who worked for you, and you were heading for disaster. His own secretary, Dorothy, was prime proof of that!

At almost fifty, over ten years his senior, Dorothy had taken on a motherly role in his life. And like most mothers with a grown-up son, she treated him with bullying affection.

However, this young woman didn't quite fit into that category! Jerome Summer was in his early fifties, and the young lady was probably only in her late twenties. Which begged the question, what role did she have in Jerome Summer's life that led to such familiarity...?

'I'll have to mention to Jerome that a flight attendant in a short skirt and silky blouse is much more conducive to comfortable travel,' Jonas said silkily.

Dark brows rose over icy green eyes as his meaning obviously became clear. 'For whom, Mr Noble?'

'Why, me, of course.' He grinned, some of the strong coffee at last seeming to kick into gear as he felt a rush of adrenaline. It would only be a temporary thing, of course, he acknowledged ruefully, but hopefully it would be long enough to get him through his meeting. 'And if, as you say, the flight is ready, where is Mr Summer?' he added frowningly. 'Or is he already on the plane?'

'Rome is at the estate, of course,' the young woman replied caustically. 'What would be the point of flying you there if Rome were already in town?' she scorned.

'Rome', was it? Jonas acknowledged sceptically. Obviously very familiar! 'I meant Danny Summer, of course,' he corrected briskly. 'I was told he would be meeting me here. He's some sort of relative, I gather?' he added hardly as the annoyance seemed to be increasing in the young woman's expression.

The mischievously slanting mouth curved. 'You gather correctly, Mr Noble,' the woman drawled. 'Do you have any luggage?'

'Only this small case.' Jonas bent down to pick up the compact black case that stood beside the chair he had been sitting in. 'I'm not expecting to stay longer than a few hours,' he added with grim determination. 'Just until my— business with Mr Summer is completed.'

Especially if all the Summer staff turned out to be as arrogantly self-assured as this young woman! He simply wasn't in the mood to bother dealing with such aggressive attitudes with any of the usual tact and diplomacy usually necessary in his work!

The young woman shot him a sidelong glance as they walked outside and in the direction of a small private jet that stood on the tarmac a few yards away. 'Exactly what line of business is it that you're in, Mr Noble?' she voiced casually.

Too casually, Jonas decided. From the little conversation they had had so far, this woman did not strike him as the sort to indulge in politeness for its own sake—which meant there had been a reason behind her question…?

'Nothing illegal, I can assure you,' he returned noncommittally.

She looked down the length of her upturned nose at him. 'You wouldn't be on your way to see Rome if it were,' she told him with disdainful certainty.

From the little he had read and heard of Jerome Summer, she was right; the man was a business legend in his own lifetime, a doctor's son who had worked his way to the top in every business enterprise he had ever been involved in.

But even so, Jonas had no intention of discussing his

business with the other man with this less-than-polite young woman!

'I'm glad about that,' he answered dismissively, grinning as he preceded her up the steps of the jet and found himself surrounded by the type of luxury he had only ever seen on celluloid before.

His own lifestyle was far from spartan, he ruefully acknowledged, but the inside of this jet was something else. It was more like a beautifully furnished sitting-room, with a comfortable cream sofa and chairs, a tan-coloured carpet on the floor, a well-equipped bar towards the cockpit. Any woodwork visible beside the doe-skin leather looked like well-polished mahogany. The only difference that he could see was that there were seat belts tucked neatly away inside the sofa and chairs.

'The bar is well stocked with food as well as drink.' The woman stood slightly behind him now, having secured the door behind them. 'Please help yourself to whatever you would like, once we have taken off, though there's a little turbulence up there today so I would advise you to wait until we've flown above it,' she added dryly as she stepped past him.

Jonas raised enquiring brows. 'And exactly what are you going to be doing while I'm helping myself to the food and drink?' he asked.

She turned in the open doorway to the cockpit, arching mischievous brows. 'Why, flying the plane, of course, Mr Noble,' she replied innocently.

She was the pilot?

To say he was surprised was an understatement—he was stunned. It had never occurred to him that—

Careful, Jonas, he inwardly taunted himself, your male chauvinism is starting to show!

But it wasn't really a question of that, he instantly defended. A male chauvinist was the last thing he was. Hell, he knew, better than most, that women were much stronger, in some senses, than men!

But this young woman had realised exactly the assumption he had made earlier in the lounge—and she had chosen to let him go on thinking it! In fact, she was still smiling her satisfaction at his mistake...

Why...?

She hadn't even known who he was when she'd come into the lounge, it had only been the fact that he'd been the only person there that had given away his identity. What had he done in the few minutes of their acquaintance to bring about such animosity?

Nothing that he was aware of. Unless...?

'Was Danny Summer not able to make the flight this morning?' he enquired lightly, looking for some sort of answer there. If this woman had been asked to pilot this flight on short notice, that could account for some of her attitude. Some of it...

Her smile faded, her mouth tight now, green eyes sparkling challengingly. '*I'm* Danie Summer, Mr Noble,' she informed him coldly. 'Jerome Summer is my father. And, to put your mind at rest,' she continued hardly as he simply stared at her, 'I'm licensed to pilot all of his private aircraft for him.'

Not just a distant relative, but the man's daughter, Jonas realised dumbfoundedly. Although how he was supposed to have realised that Danie Summer would be a woman, or indeed this particular woman, he had no idea.

He couldn't have done, he accepted, irritable at having been disconcerted in this way. And this woman—Danie Summer—had enjoyed herself enough at his expense for one day, he decided hardly.

'Then I would advise you to start piloting this one,' he

bit out harshly. 'Because my time is short, and, I believe, as valuable as your father's!'

She looked ready to pass comment on the statement, and then thought better of it, drawing in a hissing breath before going through to the cockpit, slamming the door firmly shut behind her.

Damn! Damn, damn, damn. Jonas groaned as he dropped down into one of the armchairs. He was tired, regretted ever agreeing to this appointment, especially on a Saturday, and the last thing he felt like dealing with was a woman who enjoyed nothing more than flaunting her equality, an equality that he wasn't even aware he had questioned—apart from the assumption that she had to be the flight attendant, a nagging little voice infuriatingly reminded him!—before he had even had time to indulge in a much-needed, and so far denied, late breakfast!

'Would you fasten your seat belt, Mr Noble?' her voice came coolly over the internal intercom. 'We're about to taxi for take-off.'

Jonas did as he was asked, but it did not give him a sense of well-being to know that his life was now—literally—in the hands of Danie Summer—a woman who had shown him nothing but condescending contempt so far during their acquaintance!

CHAPTER ONE

WHO was Jonas Noble?

More to the point, *what* was he?

Until a couple of hours ago, Danie had believed she had a free Saturday, had planned on having lunch with her elder sister Harrie, and Harrie's husband, Quinn McBride, before going into town to do some leisurely shopping.

But then her father had telephoned, and, despite her half-hearted objections, had managed, with his usual charming diplomacy, to talk her into flying Jonas Noble to his country estate instead.

But Rome had been less than forthcoming about his visitor, refused—again, charmingly—to be drawn as to the reason for Jonas Noble's visit.

One thing Danie hated was a mystery. And Jonas Noble himself had been no help in explaining his reason for visiting her father's home, either. He had proved just as closed-mouthed as her father when she had questioned him a few minutes ago, and his appearance was no help whatsoever in pinning down who or what he could be.

The man didn't have the look of a businessman for one thing; his dark hair was a little too long. His casual clothing—black denims teamed with a black silk shirt and grey fitted jacket—exuded none of the formal efficiency that businessmen who dealt with her father liked to adopt. Her father excluded, of course. But then, Rome was way past the stage of caring what sort of image he presented—to anyone!

Perhaps Jonas Noble was in that kind of position, too...?

Danie shook her head even as she went through the mechanics of flying; she had never heard of Jonas Noble before, and if his photograph had ever appeared in any of the business journals her father subscribed to, then Danie knew she would have remembered him. His was not a face it would be easy to forget!

It wasn't strictly a handsome face, was too angular for that; his jaw was square and determined, with a firmly sculptured mouth, and slightly aquiline nose. It was his eyes that were so arresting, Danie realised: a deep dark brown, filled with a warmth that softened all those other hard edges.

Careful, Danie, she chided herself, or you might actually start to consider Jonas Noble as an attractive man!

Well, possibly he was, she conceded, but she wasn't fooled by a man's good looks. She knew those looks invariably hid a calculating selfishness. Her experience with Ben had more than shown her—

Damn it, where had that come from? She never thought of Ben any more, considered him a part of her life that was firmly shut away from prying eyes—and prying minds. Jonas Noble was the subject under question here, not someone from her past who had cured her of wanting any romantic involvement for the last two years!

Her passenger had one piece of luggage with him, a small case, too small for a suitcase, too large to be a briefcase. So what did it contain?

Well, she wasn't going to get any answers from the man himself, she conceded wryly, so she might as well put away her curiosity until she saw her father.

She reached up to press a button above her head. 'We're levelling out now, Mr Noble,' she told him coolly over the intercom. 'This is a non-smoking flight, but please help yourself to the refreshments,' she added mockingly, a smile curving her lips as she recalled the expression on the man's face when she'd informed him she wasn't the flight attendant but the pilot! Not exactly speechless, but close enough. Obviously women didn't step too far out of their expected roles in Jonas Noble's world, Danie thought tauntingly.

But planes, and flying, had been loves of hers since she'd been a child, having travelled all over the world with her parents by the time she was five. Instead of dolls, she had had models of planes in her bedroom as she'd been growing up, rapidly progressing to ones that had worked by remote control, taking them outside and flying them for hours. Her father's pilot at the time, an older man called Edward, had been quite happy for her to accompany him in the cockpit on flights, even found a pair of overalls for her to wear so that she'd been able to help him when he'd looked in the engines.

By the time she was eighteen she had already decided exactly what she was going to do with her life. There had been a little opposition from her father, of course. But as they had recently lost her mother to cancer, those objections had been only half-hearted. Rome was so devastated by the loss. If he had thought about it at all, he would have probably expected Danie would tire of the pursuit during the months it had taken her to get her full pilot's licence, but he would have been wrong. She loved flying, it was as simple as that.

Men like Jonas Noble were a prime example of the prejudice she had come up against during the time it had taken to attain her licence! Playing at it, seemed to be most men's opinion of her chosen career, backed up, no doubt, by what they considered to be Daddy's money.

Well, she had taken enough of that over the years, Danie reflected; if she were playing at anything, it was being polite in the face of the chauvinistic intolerance she had encountered towards her chosen career from men over the last seven or eight years!

Including Ben.

Not again, she told herself impatiently. She hadn't given the man a thought for months and now she had thought of him twice in half an hour. Unacceptable!

And it was all Jonas Noble's fault, she considered. There was something about him that brought Ben to mind. She could well do without it, thank you!

She pressed the button above her head a second time. 'We will be landing in ten minutes, Mr Noble,' she told him abruptly. 'I advise you to place any debris from your food and drink in the container provided, and to fasten your seat belt.' With any luck, his visit with her father would, as he had said, be a short one, and once she had flown him back to town she might just be able to go shopping, after all!

Her father had sent Charles out in the Rolls, and not the Range Rover, to collect his guest from the private airstrip on the estate, Danie noted with some surprise as she brought the jet in to land. Curiouser and curiouser. Rome rarely used the Rolls Royce, had bought it a couple of years ago on a whim, and now considered it a little too ostentatious for his tastes. But it had been brought out of mothballs today in Jonas Noble's honour. Which again posed the question: who was he?

'Please remain in your seat until I've completely brought the aircraft to a stop, Mr Noble,' she told him brusquely over the intercom. 'I will then come back through to the cabin and open the door for you.'

She had done this trip dozens of times before, but, she

had to admit, today was the first time she had found it slightly irritating to have a conversation—one way, at that!—with an unseen person. The only consolation was that Jonas Noble probably found it just as frustrating!

Not that any frustration on Jonas's part was apparent when, a few minutes later, the plane parked on the end of the runway, she went back into the cabin area. Jonas Noble was fast asleep! From the totally relaxed look of him, he probably had been from the moment they'd taken off, Danie realised crossly.

He was still sitting in the chair he had dropped into as she'd gone through to the cockpit, although at least his seat belt was fastened. But there was no sign of him having had any of the food or drink provided, and he seemed completely unaware that they had actually landed at their destination, his lids closed, his breathing deep and even.

He looked younger in sleep than the forty or so Danie had thought him to be earlier, long dark lashes fanning out across the hardness of his cheeks, his face appearing almost boyishly handsome now that slightly mocking expression had melted from his face.

His clothes, she could see as she took her time to look at him, were tailor-made, and the black shirt was probably Indian silk. A wealthy man then?

He was really something of an enigma, Danie realised with an emotion akin to shock. Men, she had decided after her few attempts at relationships—which, for one reason or another, had always ended disastrously!—were a complete waste of her time. And she now resented having given Jonas Noble even a little of it!

She reached down and shook his arm vigorously. 'Mr Noble, we've landed—'

'I sincerely hope so,' he murmured as he opened his

eyes and looked directly up into her face. 'Otherwise there would be no one flying the plane!'

For someone who had been fast asleep seconds ago, he was a little too much awake now for Danie's liking, and she stepped back from him as if stung, putting her hands behind her back. 'There is such a thing as autopilot, Mr Noble,' she bit out in reply.

He straightened in his chair, looking out of the window beside him. 'Not when you're on the ground,' he derided, releasing his seat belt to stretch languidly.

Danie's mouth twisted even as she registered the tightening and relaxing of muscles. 'Are we keeping you up, Mr Noble?' she scorned.

He turned to look at her with brown eyes. 'As a matter of fact—yes!' He stood up. 'That half an hour is the only sleep I've had in the last twenty-four,' he explained.

Danie's eyes widened at this disclosure, her expression disapproving. 'I hope she was worth it!' It wasn't too difficult to guess that a woman would have been the reason for his lack of sleep the previous night. Those warm brown eyes hinted at a certain sensuality about Jonas Noble!

His expression softened. 'She was.' He gave an inclination of his head by way of acknowledgement. 'Now do you intend keeping me locked in here?' he enquired. 'Or do you plan on taking me to see your father some time today?'

At the taunt angry colour heightened her cheeks, and she moved to release the door, the steps sliding automatically to the tarmacked ground. 'Can you manage your luggage, or would you like me to carry it for you?' Danie did some taunting of her own.

His mouth quirked into a half-smile as he bent to retrieve the oversized briefcase from the carpeted floor. 'I can manage, thanks. And thanks, too, for a good flight,' he added lightly.

'How would you know it was good? You slept all the way through it!' she came back tartly.

He shrugged broad shoulders. 'Not until I knew we were safely up in the air,' he rejoined. 'I heard the bit about "non-smoking flight" before I zonked out. I'm afraid my earlier years spent as a junior doctor have meant I can usually sleep anywhere, at any time,' he explained apologetically.

Danie didn't hear any more of what he said after 'junior doctor'—this man was a *doctor*? And he was here to see her father? Was Rome sick?

She found that very hard to believe, had never known her father to have a day's illness in his life. But that didn't mean he was well now...

She moistened suddenly dry lips. 'And what line of medicine did you choose to specialise in, Mr Noble?' She tried to make her tone of voice interested rather than demanding—although by the guarded look that suddenly came over Jonas Noble's face, she had a feeling she had failed. Damn!

'I believe it's called "life", Danie; it's the oath all doctors take,' he returned enigmatically. 'Is that car waiting for us?' He indicated the gold-coloured Rolls Royce that was now parked feet away from the plane steps, the attentive Charles standing waiting with the back door open.

Danie flushed her irritation. 'For you,' she corrected tautly. 'I have a few things to do here before coming over to the house,' she amended reluctantly.

She would have liked nothing better than to arrive back at the house with him, to try and find out more about exactly what he was doing here. But, unfortunately, she had the plane to check over and refuelling to see to.

He nodded dismissively. 'I'll see you later, then.' He moved lightly down the steps, grinning his thanks at Charles as he got into the back of the Rolls.

Danie stood at the top of the steps and watched the car—and Jonas Noble!—drive away, her thoughts in a turmoil.

Why did Rome need to see a doctor? Obviously because he was ill, she instantly chided herself.

But to have a doctor flown out here to see him...! Was her father's illness *that* serious?

Danie suddenly felt unwell herself at the thought of that being the case. She couldn't bear the thought of anything happening to her handsome, fun-loving father.

But Jonas Noble's visit certainly appeared ominous...

'I trust you had a comfortable flight?'

Jonas looked across at his host. The older man had greeted him at the door of the manor house a few minutes earlier, and the two of them were now seated in an elegant sitting-room. He had known what Jerome Summer looked like, of course, as he had seen the other man's picture in the newspapers several times. But those photographs had only shown Rome Summer's still boyish handsomeness, despite the fact that he was in his early fifties, and couldn't possibly hint at the sheer vitality of the man.

But what did Rome expect him to say in answer to his question? The flight had been fine—it was Rome's daughter that he hadn't found comfortable.

Danie Summer—how could he possibly have known she would be female?—was as prickly as a hedgehog, with all the charm of a herd of stampeding elephants!

But she was beautiful, another little voice inside his head reminded him.

Yes, she was—if you managed to get past those prickles

and the acidic tongue! Personally, he would as soon not bother.

'Fine, thank you,' Jonas replied brusquely, waving away the offer of a cup of coffee poured from the pot on the table that stood between the two men. 'You explained the situation to me on the telephone early yesterday evening,' he continued in businesslike tones. 'So perhaps I could carry out my examination, and then we can talk some more?'

Jerome Summer didn't move, his expression agonised now, blue eyes clouded with worry. 'Before you do that, could I just stress, once again, how delicate this situation is—?'

'I've already gathered that,' Jonas assured him dryly. 'Danie doesn't know, does she?' he prompted gently.

Rome grimaced, shaking his head ruefully. 'Has my daughter been asking you awkward questions?'

Jonas shrugged. 'One or two,' he confirmed. 'Oh, don't worry,' he assured as the other man began to frown, 'a patient's confidentiality is guaranteed as far as I'm concerned.'

Rome shook his head. 'That won't stop Danie.' His frown deepened. 'Maybe it wasn't such a good idea to have her fly you here. It just seemed the best option at the time—'

'I think it's a little late in the day to worry about that,' Jonas cut in. 'Besides, Danie is your problem, not mine,' he added firmly. 'I came here to carry out an examination…?' he prompted again pointedly.

The half an hour or so of sleep he had managed to get on the plane had temporarily refreshed him, but he was no longer a young 'junior doctor' when a couple of hours sleep grabbed here and there had been enough to keep him going. At the moment the previous night's lack of rest made him feel every one of his thirty-eight years!

'I don't mean to sound terse,' he excused as he realised he had been exactly that. 'I had a difficult case to deal with last night,' he explained. 'And lack of sleep means I'm a little short on patience today!'

'Of course.' Rome Summer stood up quickly. 'I'll explain a little more to you as we go upstairs.'

Jonas picked up his case of instruments, listening politely to the other man as they ascended the stairs, realising Rome needed to talk, that he found all of this extremely difficult to deal with.

Jonas sympathised with him, could imagine how the older man must be feeling. For a man who had controlled his world, and that of his family, for the last thirty years, Jonas realised this must all have come as a bit of a shock to Rome Summer. It was something he had no control over whatsoever. But even if the other man's suspicions proved to be correct, it wasn't the end of the world. Other people, other families, had gone through this sort of thing before. And would no doubt continue to do so for a long time to come!

But Rome Summer looked less than capable of dealing with it, Jonas realised a short time later, Rome haggard now as the two men returned to the sitting-room, Jonas's diagnosis conclusive.

'I just can't believe it.' Rome groaned, his face buried in his hands. 'I had my suspicions, of course—'

'You wouldn't have telephoned me otherwise,' Jonas pointed out dryly, handing the other man a cup of the now cool coffee; in the circumstances, cold or not, the caffeine would do the other man good.

'But somehow I didn't really believe it.' Rome shook

his head dazedly, sipping the coffee without even seeming aware of what he was doing.

Jonas let the other man sit quietly for several minutes, giving him time to get over his initial shock; no doubt the coffee would help do that, too. Once the other man had accepted the diagnosis as fact, the two of them could get down to talking over the practicalities of what needed to be done over the next few months.

Rome finally raised his head, looking across at Jonas with slightly moist eyes. 'I'm sorry,' he said heavily. 'I realise I'm not taking this too well.' He gave a rueful grimace. 'I was wishing the girls' mother were here. She would have known what to do.'

'How many daughters do you have?' Jonas enquired politely, knowing the other man still needed to talk, and remembering having read somewhere that Rome Summer's wife had died several years ago.

'Just the three.' Rome sighed. 'But sometimes it seems like twenty-three!'

Jonas imagined that Danie Summer could quite easily account for twenty of those in her own right; she was certainly spirited enough to cause any man a headache, let alone her harassed father!

'Do they all live at home with you?' he asked lightly, curiosity prompting him to find out if Danie had some poor man as her husband somewhere in the background!

'None of them.' Rome shook his head. 'Harrie was married last month,' he said with obvious pleasure and pride. 'Andie is usually based in London, although she's been staying here with me the last few weeks.'

'And Danie?' Jonas persisted softly.

'I'm based, not wherever I hang my hat, but wherever I fly my aircraft!' the woman in question told him coldly as she walked unannounced into the room.

Jonas stiffened at the sound of that caustic voice, although he literally froze with shock once he had turned to look at her. The black baseball cap was gone, and he found that those dark lashes and brows had been deceptive. Hair of the most gloriously deep red now cascaded in loose waves down the length of Danie's spine.

If Jonas had thought her beautiful before, that red hair was definitely her crowning glory, giving prominence to her high cheekbones, bringing out the deep green colour of her eyes. There was no doubt about it—Danie Summer was one of the loveliest women he had ever set eyes on!

He stood up slowly. '*Your* aircraft?' he questioned silkily, feeling suddenly defensive in the face of this woman's arresting beauty.

A look of irritation darkened her features. 'Rome's aircraft,' she corrected, before turning to her father. 'Everything okay?' she prompted sharply, looking at him searchingly.

Rome seemed to have undergone a transformation in the last few seconds, Jonas noted wryly, that boyish grin back on his face, his worried expression of a few minutes ago completely dispelled. For his daughter's benefit, Jonas didn't doubt. Although there was no way Rome would be able to keep the truth from Danie indefinitely...

'Everything is fine,' Rome told Danie lightly. 'Jonas and I were just discussing having lunch before he returns to town.'

Jonas hesitated at the totally erroneous statement. Considering he hadn't even had breakfast yet...! But, he had to admit, food of any kind did sound rather tempting at the moment...

'As long as I'm not inconveniencing anyone...?' he accepted questioningly.

Glittering green eyes were turned in his direction. 'Since

when has inconveniencing someone bothered you?' Danie snapped.

Jonas's mouth firmed at the insult, Rome chuckling softly as he saw his reaction. Well, Rome might find his daughter's rudeness amusing, but Jonas found it exactly what it was—bad-mannered!

'You can have lunch with Harrie and Quinn any time, darling.' Rome put his arm lightly about his daughter's shoulders.

'But I was having lunch with them today,' Danie complained.

So she *had* had other plans for today, after all... Jonas fumed inwardly; it wasn't his fault she hadn't been able to carry them through—her father was responsible for that.

'Wouldn't you rather have lunch with two attractive men?' Rome teased his daughter.

Danie turned to give Jonas a slowly dismissive glance from head to toe. 'Not particularly,' she finally replied, before turning back to her father.

What this young lady needed was a smack on the backside, Jonas decided grimly. If her father didn't feel capable of administering it, Jonas was sure there must be plenty of other men who would!

Including him...?

Jonas frowned. He had never lifted so much as a finger against a woman in his life, and no matter how much Danie Summer might deserve a good spanking, he knew he wouldn't be the one to give it.

He had grown up in a totally female household; his mother had been widowed while still in her early thirties, and left with the sole care of Jonas and his two older sisters. Beautiful and warm-natured though she was, she had remained a widow in the succeeding years, managing, with only the help of a housekeeper, to bring the three children up alone. Meaning that Jonas, as the only male in the household, had been cosseted and spoilt by not just his mother and sisters, but the housekeeper, too.

It had been a charmed and loving childhood, instilling him with a deep respect for his mother and sisters, and a liking of women in general.

Except Danie Summer! he realised irritably.

But that, he considered, was mainly her own fault. Danie was obviously, despite her own privileged background, an accomplished and capable woman, who took her work very seriously. It was just the sharpness of her tongue that needed a little attention. A little…? Make that a lot, Jonas corrected himself firmly.

'Pity,' he drawled finally, easily able to meet the challenge in Danie's dark green eyes.

Danie's mouth twisted. 'A little sincerity wouldn't have come amiss in that statement!' she countered.

'Danie!' Rome chided. 'Must I remind you that Jonas is here as my guest?'

Jonas watched as Danie underwent a transformation, the tension leaving that beautiful face, to be replaced by a smile of gentle concern as she turned to look at her father.

Jonas felt something lurch in his chest at the difference that gentleness made to Danie; it was akin to the sun coming out in the midst of a stormy sky. And well worth waiting for, he acknowledged a little dazedly. Stripped of the cynicism that seemed to temper most of her conversation, Danie Summer was incredibly lovely.

'Perhaps lunch would be nice,' she finally conceded grudgingly. 'Would you like to freshen up before we eat, Mr Noble?' she offered with a politeness that had so far been lacking from their acquaintance.

He looked across at her with narrowed eyes, not fooled for a moment by her change in attitude, only to be met with a look of such innocence that he knew his suspicion was correct; Danie Summer had her own reason for her sudden politeness. And he had a feeling it could have something to do with the reason for his presence here today!

Well, she was wasting her time if she thought a little polite civility—something that should have been there from the beginning!—would charm out of him the reason for having come here to see her father. As he had assured Rome earlier, his relationship with his patient was always completely confidential.

As Danie Summer was going to quickly find out if she tried to pump him for information!

CHAPTER TWO

WHAT a complete waste of her time this had been, Danie muttered to herself as she pushed her food uninterestedly around her plate. She had intended originally to go upstairs and have lunch with her sister Andie. She'd only conceded to eating down here with her father and Jonas Noble in the hope of being able to find out a little more of the reason for the younger man's visit. But her father was close-mouthed on the subject, and Jonas Noble was also like a clam!

Which only succeeded in making Danie's imaginings even darker than they already were—and they were bad enough already!

Her father didn't *look* ill. A little strained perhaps, his ready smile not always reaching the warmth of his blue eyes, but other than that he seemed his normal self.

The trouble was, Danie felt so alone in her wonderings. She couldn't talk to Andie about it; her younger sister had been far from well herself since a bout of flu the previous month. Her other sister, Harrie, had only been recently married, and it would be a pity to spoil that happiness, especially if it should turn out to be unnecessary.

Audrey!

Of course, her father's assistant of the last twelve years was sure to know exactly what was going on. She might not tell Danie, perhaps, but she couldn't possibly be as clam-like as these two men had turned out to be!

'I think I'll give coffee a miss, if you don't mind.' Danie put her dessert fork neatly down on her plate before stand-

27

ing up. 'I have a few things to do before flying back this afternoon,' she told her father as he looked across at her enquiringly.

They were seated very cosily around the dining table; Danie grimaced at the scene: her father at the head, Jonas and herself sitting either side of him, facing each other across the table. Jonas's appetite, Danie had noted disgustedly, had been more than healthy in comparison with her own picking at the food. Obviously the seriousness of his work didn't affect him!

'Of course, darling,' her father accepted lightly. 'I'll give you a ring when Jonas needs to go. Oh, and I shouldn't bother to go and see Andie,' he added, looking concerned. 'She was sleeping when I called in on her room earlier.'

'Perhaps you should get Dr Noble to look at Andie before he leaves?' Danie suggested tauntingly.

'What on earth for?' her father exclaimed.

She shrugged. 'This flu seems to have been dragging on a long time. Or perhaps general medicine isn't his field?' she questioned challengingly.

Brown eyes levelly met the mockery in her gaze. 'It's been a few years,' Jonas conceded dryly. 'But I'm sure I could manage.'

'I—'

'And it's Mr Noble, Danie,' Jonas continued hardly. 'Or Jonas, if you would prefer that?'

She would prefer to know exactly what sort of doctor he was! But she knew, especially since lunch, that she would get nowhere on that subject with either of these men. A talk with Audrey definitely beckoned!

'I'll see you later—Jonas,' she dismissed him pointedly—after all, he'd called her Danie without ever having been invited to do so!

It wasn't too difficult to locate Audrey; the other woman was as much of a workaholic as Rome, busy dealing with some correspondence in his study when Danie entered there a few minutes later.

The older woman looked up with a warm smile, having become like another member of the family in the twelve years she had worked for Rome. At forty-two, she was tall, blonde, and beautiful.

'Uh-oh.' Audrey grimaced, putting aside the letter she had been working on. 'Who's been upsetting you?'

Danie scowled, sitting on the side of her father's desk. 'Is it that obvious?'

'Yes!' Audrey laughed unabashedly.

Danie chose her next words carefully. Very carefully. Because, although she knew Audrey was fond of all of them, the older woman was also completely loyal to Rome. And the last thing Audrey would ever do was break a confidence of his, business or private.

'Have you met Jonas Noble?' Danie asked lightly.

Audrey frowned. 'The man who was with Rome earlier?'

Danie looked at Audrey searchingly. Was she just delaying answering, or did she really not know anything? Danie would be surprised if it were the latter; Rome trusted his assistant implicitly. But if that should turn out to be the case... It made the whole situation seem even more ominous!

'That's the one.' She nodded casually.

'As a matter of fact, no,' Audrey replied. 'Who is he exactly?'

Danie frowned. 'I was hoping you might be able to tell me that!'

'Sorry,' Audrey said. 'But I don't have a clue.'

Damn, damn, damn! This was much worse than Danie

had thought. Never having married herself, Audrey had become one of the family, and Danie knew that Rome had absolutely no secrets from the other woman. But it now appeared Rome hadn't told Audrey anything about Jonas Noble, either...

'All I've managed to find out is that he's some sort of doctor,' she told Audrey.

'Oh,' Audrey murmured slowly.

Was it her imagination, or did Audrey's expression suddenly look guarded? But the other woman had told her she knew nothing about Jonas Noble, and Danie believed her. So why did Audrey suddenly look so wary?

'Any help?' Danie went on, watching Audrey intently.

Audrey turned away from the intensity of that searching gaze. 'Not particularly. Rome simply hasn't mentioned him.'

Rome might not have mentioned Jonas Noble, but Danie was sure that revealing his identity as a doctor had given Audrey some idea of exactly what he was doing here...

And why shouldn't it have done? Audrey spent more time with her father than anyone else, was sure to be aware if Rome was ill. Even if she wouldn't talk to anyone else about it...

Danie stood away from the desk, knowing she would get nothing further out of Audrey. 'I had better go and see if he's ready to leave yet.' She pulled a face at the prospect of spending yet more time in the company of Jonas Noble.

'Have fun,' Audrey replied distractedly, her thoughts obviously elsewhere.

Were they with Rome? Danie pondered as she walked slowly back to the dining-room. Because she had no doubt whatsoever, now that Audrey knew Jonas Noble was a doctor, she also knew exactly what he was doing here!

Danie gave an impatient sigh. If her father *was* ill, then

she had a right to know. She wasn't a child; for goodness' sake, none of them was, and, although it would be upsetting to find out Rome had serious health problems, it couldn't be any worse than how not knowing was turning out to be!

'Why the long face, Danie?' her father asked as he met her out in the hallway.

He was alone. Which posed the question; where was Jonas Noble?

Although, for the moment, Danie put that question aside, and looked intently at her father. 'What's going on, Daddy?' she demanded.

Her father steadily held her eyes. 'I—'

'And don't try and fob me off by telling me you don't know what I'm talking about,' Danie cut in determinedly, her expression mutinous. 'Because you know exactly what I meant!'

Her father raised blond brows reprovingly. 'I wasn't about to do that, Danie,' he answered softly, that very softness telling her that he was becoming angry himself. 'But I'll talk to you—to all of you—when I'm good and ready.'

Danie drew in a sharp breath. Her father was tough when it came to his business dealings, had needed to be to become the successful man he was, but he rarely, if ever, became angry with any of his daughters. The very fact that he was angry with her now told Danie just how serious this all was...

'Where's Jonas Noble?' she asked tautly.

Her father relaxed slightly, a teasing light entering the blue of his eyes. 'Unless I'm mistaken, you didn't seem in too much of a hurry to spend time in his company earlier.'

Danie grimaced. 'You weren't mistaken. But as it appears I don't have any choice in the matter—'

'Oh, but you do.' Rome grinned. 'I've had Charles drive Jonas back to London,' he explained at her sharply questioning look.

Danie blinked her surprise. Jonas Noble had already left? He was being *driven* back to town?

'And whose idea was that?' she snapped resentfully. Damn it, she might not have wanted to spend any more time in the man's company, but it would at least have given her another chance to find out more about him!

'Mine, actually,' her father replied matter-of-factly. 'Although Jonas seemed quite happy with the arrangement too,' he added.

Danie would just bet he had! She hadn't been unaware of Jonas Noble's dislike of her, knew that he had found her brash and rude. Which she had been, she conceded ruefully. But she had also been aware, when she'd entered the sitting-room before lunch, that he had been surprised by, if not attracted to, the difference in her appearance without the baseball cap, that he had been momentarily stunned by her looks. Only momentarily, she acknowledged wryly; she was sure that not too many things wrong-footed the arrogant Mr Noble for long!

'I was only talking to Audrey,' Danie muttered resentfully. 'You said you would give me a call when Jonas was ready to leave.'

Her father's humour disappeared. 'I preferred him to be driven back with Charles,' he stated firmly.

Effectively removing any chance she might have to talk to Jonas Noble again!

She didn't like this. Not one little bit. And if her father thought he had got the better of her, then he was going to be disappointed. Jonas could only have left with Charles minutes earlier, which meant they couldn't have got very far yet.

'Where are you going?' her father called after her as she turned to run up the wide staircase.

Danie glanced back only briefly. 'I think I'll go back to town too,' she told him.

'But—'

'You'll have to excuse me, Daddy,' she interrupted his protest, turning to go up the stairs two at a time. 'I'm in rather a hurry.'

It took very little time to collect the things she needed from her bedroom, and race back down the stairs again. On her way to the front door she heard the murmur of voices coming from the sitting-room.

'—will have to be told soon, Rome,' Audrey was saying gently. 'Very soon, I would have thought. This isn't something you can keep to yourself for very much longer.'

It wasn't in Danie's forthright nature to eavesdrop, but those few words held her transfixed in the hallway, her heart beating faster, her eyes dark with apprehension as she listened to the rest of what Audrey had to say.

She'd believed Audrey when the other woman had told her earlier that she didn't know who or what Jonas Noble was, or what he was doing here, but obviously the little Danie had told the other woman about him had given Audrey the answer to the latter at least...!

'I realise that,' Rome groaned in a pained voice. 'It's just that— This isn't the sort of thing you can just blurt out over breakfast one morning!' he rasped impatiently.

Audrey sighed. 'I know, but if I've been able to guess...'

'Yes, yes,' Rome muttered heavily. 'I will tell them. But in my own time,' he said grimly. 'I have to get used to the idea myself first!'

'I know, Rome,' Audrey returned huskily. 'I do know.

I just— Oh, Rome!' she choked emotionally. 'It will only be a matter of weeks before they all realise—'

'It's all right, Audrey,' Rome soothed, appearing to be the comforter now. 'It will be all right, you'll see.'

Danie couldn't stand and listen to any more, hurrying from the house, closing the door softly behind her, loath to let her father or Audrey know she had heard any of their conversation.

Weeks…! My God, did that mean—? Was her father—?

She didn't care whether Jonas Noble wanted to see her again or not—he was damn well going to. Because she was determined to get some answers from somewhere— and at the moment Jonas Noble seemed to be the man who had them all!

It was warm and comfortable in the back of the Rolls Royce, and Jonas could feel the effect of that warm comfort as his eyes once again began to close sleepily. Thank goodness it was the weekend and he could sleep in late tomorrow.

You're getting too old for this, Noble, he told himself. One sleepless night had reduced him to being almost a walking zombie. *Almost*, he smiled to himself sleepily. He had been awake enough to visit his patient today.

And he had certainly been awake enough to appreciate the beautiful, if caustic, Danie Summer!

He shook his head as it rested back against the leather seat, smiling slightly, his eyes closed. Not a woman to be trifled with, he decided, knowing that she believed he had done exactly that. And had resented him intensely for it. He—

'I'm going to pull over, Mr Noble,' Charles announced from the front of the car, glancing in his driving mirror as

Jonas opened his eyes to look across at him. 'Miss Danie seems to want a word,' Charles added helpfully.

Miss Danie—!

Jonas sat up straighter in his seat, turning to look out the back window of the car. But as far as he could see, 'Miss Danie' was nowhere to be seen. There was only a motorbike behind them, a huge monster of a black machine, with its rider bent low over the handlebars—

Jonas narrowed his eyes to look more intently at the driver of the powerful black bike, instantly recognising the deep green eyes that could be seen clearly beneath the black crash-helmet.

When she wasn't flying planes, it seemed Danie Summer rode a motorbike that looked powerful enough to crush her if it fell on her! Not that it ever would, Jonas decided; it wouldn't dare!

A woman who liked to live life dangerously, he decided.

He turned to sit patiently in the back of the car while Charles got out to talk to Danie. The back passenger door opened seconds later and Danie Summer herself climbed into the back of the vehicle to sit beside him.

Jonas raised dark brows as he looked at her. She had taken off the black helmet, releasing that cascade of flame-red hair. The black leathers she wore seemed moulded to the curves of her body—and very sexy it looked too, Jonas realised as he felt a faint stirring of his own body in response to such feminine perfection.

'To what do I owe the honour?' he prompted sarcastically, annoyed with himself for his own reaction to this woman. Beauty, he knew, was only skin deep; Danie Summer was the most outspokenly rude woman he had ever had the misfortune to meet.

Her mouth twisted derisively. 'You forgot to say goodbye,' she murmured huskily.

Jonas looked at her through narrowed lids. He didn't believe for one moment that was the reason she had followed him. Although it was becoming patently obvious that was exactly what she had done...

'Goodbye, Danie,' he said.

She smiled. 'Very politely delivered, Jonas.'

He gave an acknowledging inclination of his head. 'My mother made a point of instilling good manners into all of her children,' he returned.

Danie nodded. 'But does it have to be goodbye?' She quirked dark brows, eyes gleaming brightly.

With what, Jonas wasn't sure. A cross between challenge and flirtation, he thought; although the latter seemed unlikely in the circumstances!

He eyed her warily now. 'What did you have in mind?' he asked slowly.

Danie shrugged, colour heightening her cheekbones even as she spoke. 'I was wondering if you would have dinner with me this evening?'

Jonas drew in his breath quickly. He wasn't fooled for a moment into believing this young woman really wanted to have dinner with him—her motives for the invitation, in view of her earlier curiosity concerning the reason for his visit to her family home today, were all too obvious!— but at the same time, he was intrigued in spite of himself...

'In a word—no,' he told her bluntly, his gaze becoming amused as he saw the way angry colour suffused her cheeks now; obviously not a young lady who was used to hearing that particular word!

She swallowed hard—doing her best to swallow down a blistering response at the same time!—eyes flashing with resentment. 'Why not?' she demanded.

Jonas smiled at the return to her previous bluntness. She certainly hadn't been able to maintain that air of flirtatiousness for long! But, he realised, he thought he preferred her rudeness; it was certainly more honest, and at least he knew where he stood!

And there was no denying that Danie was amazingly beautiful...

'I wasn't saying no to dinner, Danie, just not tonight,' he heard himself say. 'It probably hasn't escaped your notice, but I'm having trouble keeping my eyes open!'

Her anger at his refusal rapidly faded, to be quickly replaced by scorn. 'Of course.' She nodded. 'You mentioned earlier that you had very little sleep last night.'

And, of course, she had already drawn her own conclusions concerning that sleeplessness.

Jonas gave an inward smile at the knowledge. Not that he hadn't had relationships in the past, and they had certainly quite often involved getting a minimum of sleep, but this particular period of time there wasn't a woman in his life. Nor had there been for some while. Mainly because he had found he was tired of relationships that seemed, ultimately, to be leading nowhere.

In fact, he had found himself doing quite a lot of soul-searching in recent months. He enjoyed his work, and good relations with his mother, and his sisters and their respective families, but just lately he had wondered if there wasn't something missing from his own life, had found himself possessed of a restlessness that neither his work nor his family could assuage.

But maybe it was the fact that there wasn't a woman in his life at the moment that had caused that restlessness in the first place!

While he didn't think having dinner with Danie Summer would help that situation, he had no doubts it would prove entertaining.

'Tomorrow evening, however, would be no problem—
if that would suit you?' he suggested.

And then wondered if he weren't making a big mistake.
While she might be breathtakingly beautiful, he hadn't particularly liked Danie Summer so far in their acquaintance,
and he was halfway sure she shared the feeling. Halfway?
Damn it, she had given every indication she heartily disliked him!

Tomorrow evening should be fun, Jonas thought. If
Danie accepted... Which, right now, she seemed to be having difficulty doing, Jonas noted shrewdly. From what
Rome had told him about his daughters, Danie wasn't married, but that didn't mean she didn't have someone in her
life. Which might make seeing him tomorrow evening
something of a problem...

Well, that was *her* problem, Jonas dismissed. If she
could offer to see him this evening, then she could make
it tomorrow evening instead.

Unless she just didn't like the delay of twenty-four
hours...?

Which was probably more than likely the case, Jonas
decided. Danie Summer had come over to him as an 'in-
stant' person. If something needed doing, then deal with it
now, not later. Which probably accounted for the way she
had followed him on her motorbike!

'Well?' he prompted impatiently; his own time, as he
had told her earlier, was no less valuable than was her own,
or her father's, and quite frankly he had used up enough
of it on this family for one day. Besides, falling into bed—
alone—beckoned.

Those green eyes flashed her anger once more before it
was quickly brought under control. Danie even went so far
as to force a smile to those poutingly inviting lips. 'Tomorrow evening will be fine,' she answered in measured

tones. 'In fact, it will probably be better,' she continued as she warmed to this change of plan—her plan! 'I'm sure I'll have no problem booking us a table at my favourite Italian restaurant on a Sunday evening.'

And Jonas was sure, if Danie decided to eat at her favourite Italian restaurant on New Year's Eve without a booking—one of the busiest evenings of the year—that a table would be found for her somehow! There was about her an assured arrogance that would ensure not too many people said that word no to her...

So it came as no surprise to him either that Danie would be the one to book the restaurant. 'What time do you intend picking me up?' he enquired tauntingly, laughing softly as she looked momentarily nonplussed at the suggestion. 'I usually call and collect the people *I've* invited out to dinner,' he informed her.

Danie looked irritated at the reminder that she had been the one to do the inviting. 'Would seven-thirty suit you?' she said tautly.

'That depends on what time you book the table for.'

Her mouth tightened at his deliberate awkwardness. 'How about eight o'clock?'

'Then seven-thirty will be fine,' Jonas returned, enjoying her momentary discomfort. Momentary—because he was sure she wouldn't remain disconcerted for long! 'In fact,' he went on softly, 'I'll look forward to it!'

It was obvious from her expression that Danie didn't share the sentiment.

Jonas laughed to himself. He did not think Danie was the answer to the restlessness that had been plaguing him recently, but she had certainly brightened up what might otherwise have been a very arduous day. In fact, he was even starting to look forward to continuing another verbal fencing-match tomorrow evening!

He glanced down at the plain gold watch on his wrist. 'If you'll excuse me, Danie,' he told her briskly. 'I have another patient to see before I call it a day.'

Impatience once again flared in those revealing green eyes at his obvious dismissal, only to be dampened down again as she made an effort not to lose the fiery temper he had already glimpsed more than once today.

'You're certainly kept busy,' she finally replied.

'Unfortunately, I don't very often get flown around in luxurious planes!'

'Where exactly do you work?' Danie asked casually.

She would never make it in the diplomatic corps, Jonas concluded; she was as transparent as glass. 'Here and there,' he answered enigmatically, having to stop himself from laughing out loud this time at the angry frustration she wasn't quick enough to hide.

'Then I had better not keep you any longer,' she said, bending to pick up her helmet and leather gloves from the carpeted floor where she had placed them earlier.

'Haven't you forgotten something?' Jonas reminded her as she threw the car door open with her usual impatience.

She turned back to him, looking puzzled. 'I don't think so…?' She shook her head, red hair framing the loveliness of her face.

So much perfect beauty, Jonas mused. What a pity her only reason for wanting to see him again was the hope of trying to get him to be less than discreet about his visit to the Summer estate today…! A wasted hope, he was afraid, but it would be interesting to see how she went about it…

'You have no idea where I live,' he told her, taking a pen and small notebook from the breast pocket of his jacket, quickly writing down his address before ripping the sheet from the pad and handing it to her. 'I'll be ready and waiting at seven-thirty tomorrow evening.'

Danie shoved the piece of paper in the pocket of her leather jacket, obviously annoyed with herself at the oversight. 'I'll try to be on time,' she snapped before getting out of the car and slamming the door shut behind her.

Charles had barely had time to get back in behind the wheel of the Rolls Royce before the black motorbike, Danie bent grimly down over the engine, shot past them with a roar, then rapidly disappeared into the distance.

Jonas relaxed back onto his seat, a smile playing about his lips. Danie Summer's tongue was as sharp as a knife, and she had an arrogance that bordered on contempt. But she was also incredibly beautiful, and the most intriguing woman Jonas had met for a very long time. If ever!

What a pity her only reason for wanting to see him again was the selfish one of wanting to know why he had been to see her father today.

And what a pity—for Danie!—that she was going to be unsuccessful!

CHAPTER THREE

'DRESSED to kill', she believed it was called. Danie studied her reflection in the mirror. The short green sequinned dress clung so lovingly to her body that she could wear only the minimum of clothing beneath it; she had dispensed with a bra altogether, and her panties were of the sheerest silk. Her hair was loose about her shoulders, like a rippling flame—red, with the merest hint of gold as it shimmered down her spine.

She had applied a little more make-up than usual, too—in fact, she didn't usually bother with it at all!—her lashes long and silky, her eyes outlined with black kohl, giving them a look of wide innocence, her cheekbones aglow with blusher, the deep red gloss on her lips a match for the colour of her hair.

If Jonas Noble didn't find her appearance attractive, then he simply wasn't a normal flesh-and-blood man!

She had been so irritated when he'd refused her invitation to dinner yesterday, even more so when he'd then suggested they meet over twenty-four hours later. She had wanted to know what was going on then, not the next day!

But, in retrospect, the delay had been fortuitous. She'd had time to calm down, to collect her thoughts, to think rationally about how she was going to go about finding out the reason for Jonas's visit to her father yesterday. And the only problem with the plan she had come up with, that she could see, was if she would be able to hold on to her temper long enough to try and seduce the information out of him!

She knew Jonas found her attractive, had seen his admiration for her looks in his face. There was no doubting the fact that he was handsome enough himself for her not to find flirting with him too arduous a task. It was the fact that he also annoyed her intensely that could pose a problem!

Besides, finding her physically attractive and actually being attracted to her as a person were two entirely different things—and Jonas had given every indication that he found her as irritating as she found him!

Not exactly a recipe for success, she acknowledged ruefully. Oh, well, she would just have to set about changing his opinion of her...

If she could have done this any other way, then she would have. She had gone back to the estate earlier today intending to talk with her father, only to find that he and Audrey had driven up to Scotland in preparation for a deal he was to complete there early tomorrow. Andie had also gone—back to her apartment in town, Danie assumed. Which was no help at all; Danie still had no intention of worrying either of her sisters with this until she was more sure of her facts.

Jonas Noble alone, it seemed, was the only person available to give her them...

Time to go, she decided firmly, picking up her small evening bag before throwing a light black cashmere wrap about her shoulders; she didn't want to add tardiness to the list of faults Jonas had no doubt already found in her!

The address he had given her was in Mayfair. But she had expected to find Jonas owned an apartment, and the tall imposing three-storey house came as something of a surprise to Danie. Obviously, whichever field of medicine Jonas Noble had chosen to go into, it was very lucrative!

Jonas looked absolutely stunning in a black dinner suit

and snowy white shirt, Danie discovered a few minutes later, when he opened the door to her ring on the doorbell!

The suit was obviously tailored to his broad shoulders, narrow waist, and long legs, the white of the shirt showing that he had a healthy tan. But it was his face, no longer looking fatigued, that took Danie's breath away, the hard planes once again softened by the warmth of his deep brown eyes.

Perhaps seducing this man wasn't going to be so easy after all—for her own peace of mind; she might actually find herself genuinely attracted to him!

'Danie Summer, I presume?' he drawled, obviously mocking the change in her appearance from her workman-like garb of yesterday.

Steady, Danie, she warned herself as she instantly felt a flash of anger at his derision. 'Jonas Noble, I presume?' she returned with dry sarcasm at the change in his own appearance.

He smiled, eyes crinkling at the corners with genuine amusement. 'You're exactly as I remembered you, Danie!'

She wished she could say the same! But now that he was no longer exhausted by lack of sleep, showered and decked out in his own finery, relaxed with the prospect of the evening ahead of them, Jonas Noble was dangerously attractive!

She gave a nod of her head. 'I'll take that as a compliment,' she returned—knowing it had been no such thing; Jonas's remark was obviously referring to the sharpness of her tongue. Then she had better not disappoint him! 'Are we going to stand here on the doorstep all evening, or are you ready to leave?'

His grin deepened. 'I wonder if you would like to come inside for a drink before going to the restaurant?'

She was disconcerted enough by the change in his appearance and demeanour without finding herself alone in this beautiful house with him. She definitely would feel more comfortable going straight to the restaurant. Although she couldn't help feeling an inner curiosity about his bachelor home...

'Perhaps we could come back for coffee after our meal?' she suggested as a compromise—if she hadn't managed to wheedle the information she wanted from him during the meal, perhaps she would stand more chance in the intimacy of his home...

'Perhaps we could,' Jonas agreed, those brown eyes seeming full of laughter now.

At her expense, Danie guessed. Could she help it if this particular man brought out every defence she possessed? Besides, he was intelligent enough to realise that her about-face yesterday had to have a motive of its own!

Which didn't bother her in the least, Danie mused on the drive to the restaurant. She would think him conceited in the extreme if he hadn't put two and two together and come up with the right answer. But he was still here, accompanying her to dinner, and that was all that mattered.

'Danie!' Marco, the Italian-born, but brought-up-in-England, owner of the restaurant greeted warmly as she entered at Jonas's side. 'It's so good to see you again. And you too, Mr Noble.' He turned to Jonas. 'I didn't realise the two of you knew each other,' he added speculatively.

'We don't,' Jonas said, shaking the other man's hand. 'Yet,' he amended with an enigmatic glance at Danie.

Danie forced the smile to remain on her lips, determined Jonas shouldn't see that his remark had caused her any alarm. Even if it had!

She had no intention of getting to know Jonas Noble, tonight or any other night, and his own professionalism should have told him that to do so would be very indiscreet. She totally dismissed the idea that she was behaving less than fairly herself. She wasn't the doctor in attendance to a member of her family, Jonas was, and if he didn't feel it was unprofessional to become intimately involved with her, then perhaps he damn well ought to!

'You are looking as beautiful as ever, Danie—'

'Cut the flattery, Marco,' she told the restaurateur shortly. 'I've had very little to eat today, and I'm starving!' she continued indelicately.

'You heard the lady, Marco,' Jonas drawled, taking a light hold of her elbow. 'I have a feeling Danie is a woman who may turn violent if she isn't fed! What do you think?' he bent to murmur softly in Danie's ear, as they followed a smiling Marco through the noisily crowded restaurant to their table.

She arched dark brows as she turned to look at him from beneath her lashes. 'I've been wondering for years why I seem to have this impatience with the rest of humanity— and you've solved the riddle for me only a short time into our acquaintance!' she said with a sweetly insincere smile.

Jonas laughed huskily. 'You only "seem" to have impatience, Danie...?' he returned pointedly.

She shrugged, moving to sit down as he held back her chair for her. 'Sometimes I'm merely baffled by their lack of imagination,' she dismissed airily.

Jonas looked admiringly at her across the width of their window table once Marco had left them to peruse the menu. 'And have you always had an answer for everything?' he finally said.

'According to my mother my first word wasn't "Daddy", it was "no"!' she told him.

A smile played about his lips now as he looked at her. 'I can believe that.' He nodded slowly. 'What was she like?'

Danie blinked her bafflement at this sudden change of subject. 'Who?'

'Your mother.' Jonas sobered. 'She must have been a pretty incredible woman to have entranced a man like Rome. And she produced some incredibly beautiful daughters, too,' he opined admiringly.

'Flattery, Jonas?' Danie taunted softly.

'Not at all,' he returned. 'Physical beauty is all too easy to see.'

'As opposed to inner beauty...?' Danie challenged.

'That's sometimes a little more difficult to find,' he acknowledged hardly.

This was all becoming a little too serious for what Danie had in mind for the evening. 'My mother was one of the lucky ones; she had inner as well as outer beauty,' she explained at Jonas's questioning look. 'She was tiny, with deep auburn hair that could look almost black in some lights, and then the fiery red of my own in sunlight. She had beautifully tiny features, almost like a doll,' Danie remembered gruffly. 'But it wasn't her looks that drew people to her.' She shook her head. 'She was one of those people who was possessed of the ability to make others happy, to only see the positive rather than the negative in people. In fact,' she added briskly, 'my mother was the complete opposite of me!'

Instead of coming back with an affirmative comment, Jonas continued to look at her for several long, timeless seconds. 'You still miss her,' he finally murmured gently.

Danie flinched, a shutter coming down over her emotions. She had been seventeen when her mother had died, had spent all of those years secure in her mother's love, within the warm glow of her mother's world of sunshine and laughter; of course she still missed her! But it wasn't something she intended discussing with Jonas!

'I would be singularly lacking in emotion if I didn't,' she answered scathingly.

Jonas nodded. 'My own mother brought my two sisters and myself up virtually alone after my father died when I was very young.'

Danie didn't want to know that, either, didn't want to know anything about his private life—it only succeeded in making Jonas seem more and more like a person in his own right. And that would never do!

'Life can be a bitch, can't it?' She was deliberately flippant. 'What do you feel like eating?' She changed the subject, lifting her own menu up in front of her face.

She was more shaken than she cared to admit by the talk of their respective mothers. She had loved her mother with an innocent completeness, and she had heard Jonas's admiration for his own mother in his one brief comment before Danie had turned to the menu so rudely.

But her own feelings about the cruel loss of her mother were other things that were locked away, only to be looked at when she was alone; she simply couldn't share them with a man she barely knew...

'Pasta, and then garlic prawns, I think,' Jonas decided before placing the menu to one side. 'If that's okay with you?' He quirked dark brows. 'There's nothing worse than having someone breathing garlic all over you when you haven't eaten the stuff yourself,' he explained at her questioning look.

Danie frowned. She had intended being friendly towards him—even if she hadn't quite managed it so far!—in order to ask him the questions she wanted answers to, but she certainly hadn't intended getting close enough for him to breathe all over her!

'Go ahead,' she answered casually. 'I was going to have the garlic mushrooms, anyway.' She made it obvious she certainly hadn't intended asking *his* permission before eating garlic!

His brown eyes gleamed with laughter as Jonas easily read her mutinous thoughts. 'And a red wine to go with it—if that's okay with you?' he enquired.

'Fine.' She put aside her own menu. 'As I'm driving I'll only be having one glass, anyway.'

'We can always get a taxi back to my house,' Jonas pointed out.

Which then posed the question; how would she get home from there...?

'I rarely drink, anyway,' she told him tautly, wondering if this man wasn't perhaps taking too much for granted by her invitation, after all...! 'And I prefer it when other people don't, either,' she added before he could comment. 'I find it tends to make people rather silly, most unlike their normal selves.'

Jonas leant towards her a little. 'Then I'm glad I don't drink alcohol in great quantities, either!'

Danie didn't see why he should be glad; so far he hadn't given any indication he cared one way or the other whether she approved of him or not.

'Please don't deny yourself the pleasure on my account,' she told him frostily.

'I wasn't about to,' he assured her before turning to order a bottle of the red wine from the waiter who had been hovering beside their table for some minutes.

Luckily the ordering of their food took some time too— time enough for the subject of Jonas's pleasure to be forgotten! She could have phrased that a little better, Danie berated herself. Although the subject of alcohol did give her another opening...

'I don't suppose it's very sensible, in your profession, to ever have too much to drink,' she voiced casually, although her gaze was narrowed sharply as she watched Jonas across the table. 'You must be constantly on call to your patients?'

Jonas appeared unfazed. 'Even doctors have some time off,' he replied.

Deliberately so, Danie was sure. 'And is tonight one of those occasions?' She made her tone deliberately light; they were at least heading in the right direction in their conversation now!

His mouth twisted ruefully. 'Unfortunately, I'm not just a doctor, Danie, I'm a consultant. I deal mainly with private patients, with fees to match. Those patients expect a personal service for those fees.'

'That sounds fair enough,' Danie agreed, anticipation beginning to well up inside her. 'Are you—?'

'Jonas!' a pleased female voice cried out in recognition.

The woman appeared to have been on her way past their table when she spotted Jonas. She was a tall, willowy blonde, her beautiful face alight with pleasure, blue eyes glowing warmly.

Jonas stood up as he recognised the other woman, the smile on his own face as warm. 'Grace!' He bent and kissed her. 'You're looking extremely well,' he told her approvingly.

The woman, Grace, looked better than 'extremely well', Danie thought irritably; she was absolutely stunningly beautiful, and her long straight hair shone like spun gold. From the familiar way Jonas had just greeted her, the two of them had—or still did—know *each other* 'extremely well'!

Wonderful. Danie had come out this evening with the purpose of wheedling information out of Jonas Noble concerning her father, and almost within minutes of their arrival it appeared they had been interrupted by a woman who obviously knew Jonas on more than a friendly basis!

It was bad enough that it was proving difficult to pin Jonas down to the conversation she really wanted to have with him, without having the woman—or one of them!—in his life interrupting them too!

Jonas's comment concerning the way Grace looked had been completely genuine, but as he turned and saw the disgusted expression on Danie Summer's face he knew that she had completely misconstrued the situation.

He gave a slight shake of his head, his mouth thinning at the accusation he could read in Danie's eyes. His annoyance at that accusing look wasn't helped by the fact that ordinarily he would have felt no compunction about explaining his acquaintance with Grace. But, in the present circumstances, he simply couldn't do that...

'Danie Summer, this is Grace Cowley,' he introduced stiffly. 'Danie is a friend of mine, Grace,' he explained, knowing Danie—sharply astute Danie!—wouldn't fail to pick up the fact that he hadn't said what part Grace played in his life.

Because he had no intention of explaining that to Danie. She was bright and intelligent, and, once an explanation was given as to how he had first become acquainted professionally with Grace, Danie would put two and two together and come up with the correct answer of four! He had to remember that a patient's privacy, albeit that of a member of Danie's family, was at stake here...

'How lovely,' Grace greeted Danie with warm sincerity. 'It's way past time some lucky woman snapped this gorgeous man up and made a family man out of him!' The last was accompanied with a merry look in Jonas's direction.

He smiled in appreciation of the suggestion, knowing his bachelorhood was considered a challenge by the majority of women in his acquaintance; the married ones tried to set him up with single female friends of theirs, and the single ones thought he was fair game.

'I'll marry when I'm good and ready,' he said firmly. 'How are Gerald and the family?' he went on, knowing by her tense expression that Danie was listening avidly to every word of this conversation. Probably hoping to pick up some snippet of information on him that she could use once they were alone together again!

'Gerald is sitting over there.' Grace turned and waved across the restaurant at her husband. 'And the twins are doing marvellously. Growing fast, of course,' she added wistfully. 'You must come and see us all some time,' Grace encouraged determinedly.

'I'll do that,' he returned noncommittally. 'Now, we really mustn't keep you from Gerald any longer...'

Grace gave a throatily appreciative laugh. 'I can take the hint that the two of you want to be alone!' She reached up and kissed Jonas on the cheek. 'Nice to have met you, Danie.' She smiled. 'And remember, Jonas, I love weddings.' At that, Grace wended her way back to the table where her husband waited.

Jonas sat down, deliberately avoiding looking at Danie, although he could feel her scathing glance on him. She had obviously drawn her own conclusions about his relationship with Grace, regardless of her husband and children.

Damn it, he wasn't going to disabuse Danie of those assumptions! Why should he? Besides, he simply couldn't, not without breaching a professional confidence...

Danie's mouth pursed at his continued silence. 'What an absolutely beautiful woman,' she commented.

'Absolutely,' he answered tersely.

'I—'

'Our first course appears to be arriving,' Jonas interrupted thankfully, sitting back to let the waiter put their respective plates in front of them.

Danie looked irritated by the interruption, and picked listlessly at her food, clearly having little interest in what she ate.

In contrast Jonas enjoyed every mouthful of his own starter with apparent relish. He hadn't been needed at the clinic today, giving him a chance to catch up on chores that had necessarily to be put off until the weekend, and as a consequence he had eaten very little all day.

'Obviously being in the company of a beautiful woman gives you an appetite,' Danie suddenly bit out tartly. 'I wasn't referring to me!' she exclaimed as he raised his eyebrows.

He glanced across the restaurant. 'Grace is beautiful, isn't she?' he acknowledged clinically. 'She's also very happily married.'

Danie looked sceptical. 'But obviously that wasn't always the case.'

Jonas sighed. 'It has been during our acquaintance. Look, Danie—'

'Hey, it's none of my business.' She made an obvious effort to dismiss it lightly. 'What happens in your private life is your own affair—'

'This dinner is taking place in my private life,' he interrupted.

'Not exactly.' Danie gave a laugh. 'We met in your professional life.

'The two are completely separate as far as I'm concerned,' Jonas told her.

'Are you telling me the two never overlap?' Danie looked at him with assessing eyes.

'Never,' Jonas answered firmly.

She was far from happy at his reply, he could see. But he couldn't help that. It was the truth; he never mixed his professional life with his private one. He had agreed to have dinner this evening with Danie Summer, not with the relation of his patient, and the sooner Danie accepted that the better!

He sat forward in his seat, reaching across the table to touch her hand where she distractedly crumbled her bread roll on the plate at her side, his clasp tightening on hers as she tried to remove her hand from his. 'I'm having dinner with *you*, Danie, not your family,' he murmured huskily. 'Can we just leave it at that?'

'But—'

'Who knows?' he said teasingly. 'If we forget all about how we met yesterday, you may just find you start to enjoy yourself!'

From the look on her face—frustration mingled with anger—there didn't look as if there was too much chance of that!

Which was a pity. Because he was actually starting to enjoy this verbal fencing-match with Danie Summer. Not only was she an amazingly beautiful woman herself, but, once you got past that brittle shell, she was also bright and intelligent.

A highly lethal combination as far as he was concerned, Jonas was quickly discovering!

CHAPTER FOUR

DANIE studied Jonas disgruntledly beneath lowered dark lashes as she ate her main course. It hadn't changed: clams *couldn't* be any more close-mouthed than he was turning out to be. Whatever direction she approached the subject of his work from, somehow he seemed to avoid giving her an answer. Which, from her point of view, made this dinner a complete waste of time!

Except...

She didn't know what she had expected of this evening, but actually finding herself attracted to Jonas Noble certainly hadn't been part of the plan!

His physical good looks weren't in doubt, those warm brown eyes like hot molasses. But she was quickly discovering that he was also wittily charming, and that he had an integrity where his work was concerned which, while being irritating in her case, was nevertheless admirable in this day and age.

The truth of the matter was, Jonas Noble was the most attractive and interesting man she had met in a very long time—if ever!

'Care to share the reason for the smile?'

She gave Jonas a startled look—she hadn't realised she had been smiling. What was there to smile about in finding this man attractive? Her experience of men so far had taught her that first impressions were usually the wrong ones!

Except... This was her second opinion where Jonas was

concerned, a little voice mocked inside her head; her first had been much less flattering!

But after Ben she no longer trusted her own opinions where men were concerned—second, third, or fourth! Jonas appeared to be a highly eligible bachelor, charming, successful, rich, but that didn't mean that was what he actually was.

Coward, that voice mocked again.

Well, she couldn't help it; experience had taught her never to take anything or anyone at face value. Besides, Jonas was far from forthcoming in one particular area of his life!

'Not really,' she snipped. 'How's your food?'

'Excellent. As usual,' Jonas answered smoothly.

Danie nodded. 'Marco obviously knows you quite well.'

'Quite well, yes,' Jonas confirmed enigmatically.

And as it wasn't the sort of restaurant where one ate alone, that posed the question: who did Jonas usually come here with? It would be a woman, of course. Maybe even the beautiful Grace—before her marriage, of course, Danie allowed. He—

'My youngest sister,' Jonas said softly.

Once again Danie gave him a startled look, this time mixed with irritation. 'What about her?'

'You were wondering who I've been here with in the past; the answer is, my youngest sister,' he repeated.

Danie felt the warmth that coloured her cheeks. Was she that transparent? If she was, she was losing it; most people claimed she was extremely difficult to know. Maybe they had just meant that literally, she wondered self-derisively; she knew her brittle sense of humour certainly wasn't everybody's cup of tea!

'We came here together a lot after her separation and subsequent divorce,' Jonas explained.

'I'm sorry,' Danie murmured politely. Divorce was so common nowadays, it was coming to be a pleasant surprise to see a marriage that was surviving!

Her feelings were jaundiced, she knew that, but nevertheless she had decided long ago that if she couldn't have the sort of marriage her parents had had together, then she didn't want to bother. And so far none of the men she had met had even remotely changed that opinion.

Except Ben... But, in retrospect, he had turned out to be even more dishonest than most.

Were there no men left in the world who wanted a one-to-one relationship, who would return the kind of love Danie knew she was capable of giving herself? Again, her experience had told her no.

'I'm not,' Jonas answered her. 'Her husband was a first-class bastard; she's well rid of him.' The warmth had gone from those brown eyes now, to be replaced with a cold implacability.

This was a side of Jonas that Danie hadn't seen before, giving his character a new dimension. But it wasn't one she disliked. His obvious anger towards his ex-brother-in-law spoke of strong family ties—something else most men seemed to be lacking in nowadays. It seemed to be an utterly 'me' culture at the moment, and it wasn't one that Danie particularly admired.

She gave Jonas a warm smile. 'I'm sure your sister was glad of your love and support during such a difficult time.'

Jonas gave her a sharply searching glance, as if he suspected her of mockery.

Danie met that gaze for long, timeless seconds. 'I come from a close family myself, remember, Jonas?' she finally said.

He relaxed slightly. 'So you do,' he drawled. 'We've

come back full circle to the reason you invited me out to dinner, haven't we?' he mocked lightly.

Her smile became guilty now. 'Was I that obvious?'

Jonas chuckled, relaxing back in his seat. 'You were,' he confirmed without rancour. 'How do you think you're doing so far?'

'Lousy!' she acknowledged with a self-deriding grimace. 'You're better at this than I am.'

Once again he reached out and touched her hand. 'I don't mean to be obstructive, Danie,' he apologised. 'It's fine for us to have dinner together, but you have to understand—I have no choice but to respect my patient's privacy.'

'Even with the relatives of that patient?' she persisted intensely, making no move to take her hand from beneath his.

'Especially then,' Jonas replied quietly. 'On the basis that if my patient wanted you to know then they would tell you.'

Danie felt a flash of anger at this logic, but it was quickly followed by a grudging return of respect for this man seated opposite her. He was telling her as gently as he could that he wasn't going to reveal anything, no matter what methods of persuasion she might try to bring into play! And she could hardly criticise him for one of the qualities she was learning to admire in him.

Although she wasn't sure admiring Jonas Noble was a good idea. Because with a man who looked like this, was as charming as this, it wouldn't stop there. A relationship between the two of them, in the circumstances, was surely going nowhere. She—

'Don't analyse things so much, Danie,' Jonas cut in huskily on her thoughts, his thumb moving caressingly across the back of her hand. 'Have you never thought of just letting life run its course?'

'Several times.' Now she did remove her hand from under his, although the tingling sensation his touch had aroused continued long after she had thrust it beneath the table. 'It was always disastrous!'

Jonas sat back with a laugh. 'Maybe your judgement has just been at fault.'

'Maybe it still is,' Danie rejoined.

'I can't argue with the logic of that,' Jonas mused.

She looked across at him keenly. 'Have you ever been married?'

'Have you?' he came back smoothly.

'Certainly not!' she snapped.

'Why not?'

Danie frowned at his persistence. 'Why haven't you?' She wasn't even sure he hadn't been, but she felt slightly under attack by this line of questioning.

He shrugged his broad shoulders. 'Simple enough. I haven't found the right woman yet.'

'The right woman?' she repeated dazedly.

'Of course,' Jonas replied.

Danie stared at him. The right woman! Was he serious?

Jonas chuckled once again. 'Don't look so horrified, Danie.' He grinned. 'I'm one of the old-fashioned breed, I'm afraid. One man, one woman. As long as—'

'She's the right one,' Danie finished for him huskily, unable to tear her gaze away from him now.

And she wasn't horrified. Far from it. His words had just echoed her own thoughts...

This man couldn't be for real—could he?

'And until I find her,' Jonas continued lightly, 'I'm quite happy in my bachelor state.'

No doubt he was, with beautiful women like Grace in his life!

She was being unfair now, Danie castigated herself. The man had just echoed her own feelings, and all she could do was question his statement. Had her cynicism really become that entrenched?

'You haven't told me yet why *you've* never married,' Jonas said.

There was no way she was going to admit that it was for the very same reason *he* hadn't! 'Haven't you noticed, Jonas? I'm a pilot,' she returned. 'And in my job I fly whenever and wherever my father wants to go; there can't be too many men that would have patience with that!'

'Why not? You would have been a pilot when they met you, a relationship shouldn't make you less than you are.'

Again Danie wondered, was this man for real? Besides, it was easy to theorise about such a situation, but the reality of it was much different.

'Would you be tolerant of a woman's career?' she asked disbelievingly.

'I'm not *that* old-fashioned, Danie!' he rebuked her. 'And I'm not saying it would be easy,' he answered seriously. 'But if you love someone—'

'You can work these things out,' Danie finished scathingly. 'The words are easy to say, Jonas, actually doing it is something else entirely.'

He remained relaxed. 'As I said, it wouldn't be easy. But I wouldn't expect to give up being a—my career,' he corrected. 'So why should I expect my wife to do so?'

Danie shook her head. 'As I said, Jonas, words. It's all just words.'

'At the moment, yes, but I hope I'm big enough to put it into practice one day. I— Would you like dessert, Danie?' Jonas offered as the waiter returned to their table.

'I'm not really a dessert person,' she refused reluctantly. Because she wasn't at all anxious for this evening to end just yet, not when the conversation had just become so interesting!

'Me neither.' Jonas smiled up at the waiter. 'Just the bill, thanks.'

'No coffee?' Danie prompted once the waiter had departed.

'My place, remember?'

Vaguely, she did. But while it had seemed a good idea earlier as a last-ditch attempt to prise some information out of him, she was no longer sure it was a good idea for her to go back to this man's home with him. No longer sure at all...

'Thank you.' Danie waylaid the waiter as he returned and would have handed Jonas the bill.

'Danie—'

'*I* invited *you* out to dinner, Jonas—remember?' she deliberately used the same word he had a moment ago.

Those brown eyes glowed warmly. 'I remember, Danie. How could I forget? It's the first time a woman has ever invited me out rather than the other way round!'

'Really?' Danie smiled as she took her credit card from her small bag and handed it to the waiter; she was glad she was a first at something for Jonas.

'Really.' Jonas returned her smile.

They were becoming altogether too friendly, Danie realised with a start. Actually coming to really like each other hadn't been something she had envisaged when she had made that invitation.

Or maybe it was the effect of the red wine? No... She had kept to the one glass, as she had said she would, and Jonas hadn't drunk much more than that himself.

Damn—they really did like each other!

'Would you return the compliment and come out to dinner with me one evening this week?' Jonas cut in softly on her chaotic thoughts.

She swallowed hard. A second dinner together? They hadn't got through the first one yet!

'Aren't you being a little optimistic, Jonas?' she parried. 'We still have a way to go on this one yet!'

'So we do,' he laughed. 'But I have to tell you, I've enjoyed it this far!'

So had she. In fact, for the most part she had forgotten the purpose of the evening altogether. Which was a terrible admission, she thought self-disgustedly.

She wanted to know what was wrong with her father, not—not—not to stand on the brink of an affair with Jonas Noble!

Because that was what was happening here. She knew it as surely as if they had spoken the words out loud. Jonas was as aware of her as she was of him. And that could lead to only one conclusion.

Help!

Once that defensive wall was allowed to slip, she *was* transparent as glass, Jonas realised tenderly. And maybe that was the reason she had built that wall in the first place? It couldn't have been all that easy being one of Rome Summer's daughters, with all the wealth it involved, both now and in the future, when your emotions were there for everyone to see!

Whatever the reason for that wall, Jonas appreciated the fact that for some reason he was being allowed to see behind it. And to realise that Danie's sharp wit and sarcastic manner were part of the shield she used to hide her much softer nature.

And—

'I'm ready to leave whenever you are,' Danie told him tersely once the waiter had returned her card to her.

He had no doubt the wall wouldn't remain down for very much longer, Jonas inwardly finished.

Danie was a very private person, and no doubt she felt she had already shared enough of that softer side of herself for one evening. Besides, she was obviously also wary of the physical awareness that seemed to have sprung up between them during the evening.

Well, he couldn't exactly say he was overjoyed by it himself!

He had always preferred tiny, kittenish women, like his mother and sisters, women he could relax with—and instead he found himself attracted to an almost-six-foot-tall red-haired Amazon, with all the relaxing qualities of a charging tiger!

He shook his head ruefully as the two of them walked across the restaurant side by side, shocked for a brief moment when he caught sight of their reflection in one of the long mirrors that adorned the walls: they made a stunning couple.

'Don't analyse things so much, Jonas,' Danie tauntingly returned his earlier advice to her as she moved assuredly across the car park to unlock her car. 'Just let things run their course,' she added as she held the passenger door open for him with a flourish.

That was the basic trouble—in the circumstances, what possible course could there be for the two of them?

He paused by the open car door. 'Thanks for the advice, Danie.' He bent to briefly brush his lips across hers, raising his head to look down in the semi-darkness at her suddenly flushed face. 'Let's hope it doesn't lead us *both* into disaster!' he murmured before sliding into the low passenger seat of her sports car.

This woman seemed to like speed: planes, motorbikes, sports cars. Maybe she hoped that if she just kept running fast enough no one—no *man*, Jonas corrected himself— would ever catch up with her.

He sighed heavily as her anger at his audacity in kissing her manifested itself in the slamming of the car door behind him before she marched round to her own side of the car and got in behind the wheel.

Well, he had been curious to see what her reaction would be to his kissing her—and as she accelerated the car with a roar out onto the road, pressing him sharply back against the leather seat, he knew that she was absolutely furious at the liberty.

'Never offer others advice you can't follow yourself,' he pronounced as the car raced assuredly through the evening traffic. 'And this is a thirty-mile-an-hour zone, Danie,' he added, the speedometer showing she was doing fifty.

To her credit she did slow the car down to the appropriate speed, but the mutinously angry expression remained on her face, those cat-like eyes seeming to shoot green sparks.

Jonas continued to watch her in the semi-darkness of the lit streets that led to his house. The phrase 'you look beautiful when you're angry' sprang to mind—but, as he wanted to retain his own teeth, he wisely kept quiet. Even if it were the truth!

'Coming in for that coffee?' he asked once Danie had brought the car to a screeching halt only feet away from his front door.

At least she had stopped the car—he had been beginning to wonder!

Plainly, she also fought an inner battle with herself before answering him. He could sense her dogged curiosity was at war with those alarm bells ringing in her brain that told her to get as far away from him as possible!

Jonas held his breath as he waited for her answer, knowing that if she decided to accept his invitation it could change things between them, irrevocably.

'Coffee sounds—good,' she finally answered stiltedly.

Don't expect anything else, her tone was telling him, Jonas realised with amusement. Although why he should be amused, he had no idea; he didn't particularly like the idea that she believed he would take the invitation a step further and try to seduce her into bed.

There was no doubting Danie's beauty, or that he was very attracted to her; he just felt he should have more than a few hours' acquaintance with a woman before attempting to make love to her. Why, he hoped that, even in his student days, he had had a little more finesse than that!

'I've had no complaints so far,' he said curtly, ignoring the sharp look she gave him as he stepped out of the car.

He unlocked the front door, switching on the lights as he made his way assuredly to the kitchen through the silence of the house, Danie trailing behind him.

He had had a cook-cum-housekeeper for a short time several years ago, but his work was such that he was never sure when or if he would be home for meals, and after several weeks of ruined or uneaten food the housekeeper had predictably handed in her notice. Never to be replaced. He liked his privacy, he had decided, was quite capable of cooking his own meals if necessary, and a daily cleaner took care of that side of things.

'Have a seat while I make the coffee,' he advised Danie, moving capably about the kitchen as he prepared the coffee-machine.

'You've done this before,' Danie observed dryly, watching him as she sat at the pine kitchen table.

Jonas turned to her with raised brows. 'Done what before?' he said innocently.

Colour darkened her cheeks, and she sat up straighter in her chair. 'Made coffee, of course,' she returned shortly.

Jonas smiled before turning back to the coffee preparation. He couldn't help it. Danie, whether caustic or sweetness itself—and the latter didn't happen too often, he had to admit!—had the ability to make him smile.

'Do you live here alone?'

Her tone, Jonas surmised, was deliberately light, which probably meant it had never occurred to her that he wouldn't have at least a housekeeper to take care of his needs. In other words, she hadn't expected to be completely alone here with him!

'Completely,' he drawled unconcernedly, turning to look at her with laughing brown eyes, the coffee-machine now bubbling away nicely behind him.

She moistened red-painted lips. 'How on earth do you manage?'

'A man alone, and all that?' Jonas queried amiably. 'As it happens, I'm pretty self-sufficient, quite capable of washing and cooking for myself.'

'I find that surprising. Having been brought up by your mother and two older sisters,' Danie explained at his questioning look.

Jonas grinned. 'My mother made it plain to me, as soon as I was old enough to understand, that women were not put on this earth solely to cater to a man's needs!' He laughed at Danie's wide-eyed expression. 'She was right, of course.'

'She sounds—'

'Very forward-thinking,' Jonas finished affectionately. 'She still is.'

'I was going to say she sounds wonderful,' Danie corrected.

'She's that too,' Jonas agreed warmly. 'Once my sisters and myself were old enough to be left she took herself off to university, got a degree in history, before going on to teach. She only retired last year,' he added proudly.

Because he *was* immensely proud of his mother. A lot of women in her position, widowed with three children, would have chosen a much less productive avenue. But Jeanette Noble was made of much sterner stuff. Hopefully, her children had inherited that steely backbone.

'She's the reason you have such a tolerant attitude towards women having careers of their own,' Danie realised knowingly.

'Partly,' he acknowledged, pouring their coffee. 'Shall we go through to the sitting-room with this?' He held up the tray of coffee things.

Danie looked disappointed. 'It's quite cosy in here.'

Too cosy, Jonas was quickly discovering. The kitchen, as the heart of his home, was encircling them in an intimacy he wasn't sure Danie was ready for—and he knew he wasn't! Damn it, the woman had only invited him out in the first place because she wanted to know the reason for his being at her family home yesterday.

'If you're cold I'll put the fire on for you in the sitting-room,' he told her, not waiting for her to answer before leading the way through to the sitting-room and, as good as his word once he had put down the tray, flicking the switch on the gas fire.

Danie was staring curiously around the room when he straightened to look at her, taking in the relaxing cream and gold decor, the mahogany furniture, her gaze coming to rest on the piano that stood near the French doors that led out into the garden.

'Do you play—or is it just somewhere for you to put your photographs?' She dryly referred to the dozens of framed photographs that stood on the piano's top.

'I play,' Jonas ventured. 'But very seldom, so it's also somewhere for me to put photographs!'

Danie strolled over to the piano, tall and graceful in her clinging green gown, having left her wrap in the car. 'You must have dozens of relatives,' she said admiringly.

'Actually, no.' Jonas walked over to join her beside the piano. 'My sisters are extremely doting mothers, and, as I'm godfather to all their children, I receive a deluge of photographs of the little darlings every Christmas and birthday—mine as well as theirs! They would notice if even one of those photographs were missing.'

Danie turned to smile up at him. 'You know you love it,' she teased laughingly.

Jonas smiled back at her. 'I cannot tell a lie...' he murmured huskily, knowing a sudden awareness of Danie as she stood only inches away from him. He had only to reach out and—

Danie's eyes widened in alarm before she quickly turned back to the photographs, obviously as aware of Jonas in that moment as he was of her. And she was not at all happy about it!

Her hair smelt of lemons, Jonas discovered as he moved slightly closer, admiring its silkiness, aching to run his fingers through that molten flame. As she gave a nervous glance back at him he knew he wanted to taste her lips too, to drink in that pouting loveliness, to—

'Don't, Jonas,' she groaned throatily.

He hadn't been aware of it, but his actions had followed his thoughts, and he found himself coming to a halt with his lips only centimetres away from Danie's. 'Why not?'

he asked gruffly, their breaths mingling warmly as he looked straight into those alarmed green eyes.

She swallowed hard. 'Because—because— What about that patient confidentiality you talked about?'

'Not good enough, Danie. You're not my patient. And it was far, far too slow in coming,' he murmured softly before his lips gently claimed hers.

She tasted of fruit and honey, and as his arms moved about the slenderness of her body, moulding those soft curves to his much harder ones, it was as if the other half of himself had finally been put in place.

Jonas wrenched his mouth from Danie's, looking down at her disbelievingly. He didn't really know this woman—

So what? a little voice mocked inside his head; he might not know her, but his body certainly did!

Physical attraction, that was all it was, he told himself firmly. And he was past the age of wanting a relationship based only on that.

Only...?

Yes, only!

He turned away abruptly to move over to the low table to pour their coffee into the waiting cups. The sooner this was drunk, then the sooner Danie Summer would leave. And that was something he knew she had to do. Very soon!

He glanced across at her. Her face was turned away from him as she once again looked down at the photographs on the piano top. But even so he could see how pale her cheeks now were, green eyes huge against her pallor.

Jonas straightened slowly, frowning across at her. 'Danie—'

'I have to go!' she told him sharply, avoiding his gaze as she quickly crossed the room.

'Danie...?' He reached out and grasped her arm as she would have walked straight past him to the door.

She tossed back flaming red hair as she looked up at him challengingly, green eyes flashing her anger. 'I said I have to go, Jonas,' she bit out tautly, looking down pointedly at his firm grasp on her upper arm.

Jonas's frown deepened. 'It was a kiss, Danie. The customary thank-you at the end of a pleasant evening. Nothing more. Nothing less,' he added, not sure himself if that was strictly accurate.

It might have started out that way, but he had quickly discovered there had been a lot more to that kiss than a thank-you. Which was the reason it had come to such an abrupt end!

Danie's mouth tightened. 'The words would have been sufficient!'

Maybe so—they would certainly have been less disturbing! But now that it had come time for Danie to leave, Jonas found that he couldn't let her do so without knowing he was going to see her again. And he didn't mean at her father's home when he revisited his patient!

Jonas retained his hold on Danie's arm. 'You haven't given me an answer concerning our having dinner together again some time this week,' he reminded huskily.

Her throat moved convulsively. 'I don't think that would be a good idea, do you?' she finally returned gruffly.

'Caution seems to be something that disappeared from my thought processes the moment I met you!'

Danie again swallowed hard, wrenching her arm free in such a way Jonas was sure it must have hurt her. Although she gave no sign of that as she gave him a hard look. 'Then it's as well I've maintained mine,' she bit out. 'To me you're only my father's doctor, Jonas, with information that I want, but that you refuse to give me. As far as I'm concerned this is the end of our acquaintance,' she told him coldly.

Jonas knew she was being deliberately rude, and he could take an educated guess that it was the kiss they had just shared that had caused this knee-jerk reaction. Rationally he could reason all that out—but that still didn't mean he was unaffected by her deliberate nastiness!

'Do I take it that's a no to dinner?' he rasped with obvious sarcasm.

She had the grace to blush in the face of what they both knew to be her ill-mannered behaviour, sighing heavily. 'I just don't think it would be a good idea, Jonas, for us to—'

'Confirmation of your refusal will suffice, Danie,' he cut in.

Her gaze dropped from his. 'My answer is no, Jonas,' she said a little shakily. 'I—I have to go. I— My wrap…?' She looked about her agitatedly.

'You left it in the car,' Jonas told her flatly.

'Fine. Then—goodbye, Jonas,' she told him before hurrying from the room, the front door to the house closing behind her seconds later, to be quickly followed by the roar of the car engine as she drove away.

Jonas dropped down into one of the armchairs, brooding darkly. Not the most successful evening he had ever had, he acknowledged.

But he would see Danie again. And very shortly, if he weren't mistaken.

Because there had been something completely unbelievable about her earlier statement concerning his visit to her father yesterday. Once she discovered the truth of that, Jonas had a feeling he would see Danie again. Probably with all guns blazing!

CHAPTER FIVE

'BETTER late than never, I suppose,' Harrie said merrily as she sat down opposite Danie at the restaurant table. 'And so much nicer to eat out.' Danie's older sister looked about them appreciatively. 'I feel quite sorry for Quinn, having to miss out on this treat,' she chattered on, seeming to have no idea of Danie's misery as she sat listening to her. 'Although not too much, of course,' Harrie laughed. 'It will be nice to have a girlie chat before Quinn and I go away tomorrow for a few days— Good grief, Danie; what on earth is the matter?' Harrie exclaimed as she finally became aware of Danie's lack of input into the conversation. 'You look as if you've found a pound but actually lost five!'

Probably because that was exactly how she felt, Danie acknowledged to herself heavily. She had finally met a man she admired as well as felt half in love with already— and after Sunday evening she knew he was as far removed from her as the stars in the sky.

She had felt totally miserable about the whole affair the last day or so, finally knowing she had to talk to someone about it. She had always been close to Harrie...

'Harrie, I think I'm in love.' She attempted to add a smile to the starkness of that statement, but knew she had failed in that attempt as it came out as more of a grimace than anything else.

'But that's wonderful— No, it isn't, is it?' Harrie said slowly, looking concerned once more at Danie's misery.

72

'If it were, you would look a damn sight more cheerful than you do! It isn't another Ben, is it, Dan—?'

'Certainly not!' she cut in sharply. 'Although it might just as well be,' she added emotionally. 'I—' She broke off as the waiter hovered near their table waiting to take their order. 'Shall we have a bottle of wine?' she suggested agitatedly, the mere mention of Ben throwing her into renewed misery.

'A bottle of Chablis, please,' Harrie told the waiter lightly before turning back to Danie. 'This one hasn't driven you to drink, has he?'

Danie gave a humourless smile. 'He hasn't driven me to anything.' Literally. Because so far in their acquaintance she had flown and driven Jonas wherever they had gone together!

'Then what—?' Harrie broke off the conversation again as the waiter reappeared efficiently with the requested bottle of wine, pouring some out into a glass for each of them before disappearing again. 'Sometimes they can be a little too attentive,' Harrie observed.

Danie took a sip of her wine. The last day or so had been awful, as far as she was concerned, but now that it actually came to it she wasn't sure what to say to Harrie. Not without bringing their father into the conversation, and she had no intention of doing that...

'So who is he?' her older sister probed. 'And why do you look so unhappy?'

Instead of ecstatic, as a woman in love should be, Danie accepted. It wasn't as if Jonas didn't find her attractive, or want to see her again, because she was sure that he did, on both counts. There were just reasons why that could never be. After Jonas's reassurances on Sunday evening they had nothing whatsoever to do with his professional relationship with her father.

She drew in a ragged breath. 'You know the reason I broke up with Ben—'

'But you just said this situation wasn't—like that,' Harrie reminded her.

'Jonas isn't married, that's true.' Danie sighed, knowing her sister still hesitated to mention that was the reason Danie had stopped seeing Ben Trainer.

Not that she had known he was married when she'd gone out with him; that knowledge had come much later in their relationship.

It had all seemed so idyllic at first; Ben was a television interviewer who had come to talk to her father concerning appearing on his current affairs programme. Ben was tall, and dark, with wickedly teasing blue eyes; Danie had been attracted to him from the first, more than happy to accept when he'd invited her out to dinner.

The weeks that had followed had been some of the happiest she had ever known, Ben being an amusing as well as attentive companion. The end had come the day she'd walked into a restaurant and seen him seated at a table with a pretty blonde woman, the two of them obviously well acquainted and in deep conversation.

Nevertheless, Danie, in her innocence, had made her excuses to her sister Andie and crossed the restaurant to say hello to Ben. Only to find herself being introduced to his wife, Nikki!

Danie had looked at Ben in stunned disbelief before beating a hasty retreat, grasping Andie's arm as she'd told her sister they were going to eat somewhere else.

Of course, Ben had called round to her apartment that evening, full of excuses and apologies, insisting that Nikki was his wife, but that the two of them had been parted for months, that they had actually been discussing their divorce and the arrangements for the children when Danie had seen them together.

Danie hadn't believed him; she hadn't believed him for a very good reason. She had seen the look of pain and disillusionment on Nikki Trainer's face as Danie had greeted Ben with intimate warmth, knew that the other woman had guessed at the relationship between the two of them. And been totally devastated at the realisation!

Danie had also seen Nikki Trainer's face on Sunday evening, in several of the family photographs that stood on top of Jonas's piano! She didn't need to be told that Nikki Trainer was the youngest sister he had talked about. The one that had divorced her husband…!

Danie cringed as she recalled her shock on seeing those photographs at Jonas's on Sunday evening. For the second time in her life she hadn't been able to get out of a place fast enough—and Ben Trainer was responsible for both of those times.

Jonas had described his ex-brother-in-law as a 'bastard'—but somehow Danie had the feeling that he didn't yet know about her own unfortunate relationship with Ben. Nikki Trainer obviously hadn't regaled her big brother with all the messy details!

How would Jonas react to being told she had been involved with the 'first-class bastard'?

Danie didn't even want to think about it!

Just as she dared not go out with Jonas again. Because she had no doubts she was falling in love with him. And if, by some miracle, he should ever learn to return those feelings, he would want to introduce her to his family, to his sister, Nikki…!

Danie knew she was thinking way ahead of where she was now with Jonas, but even the possibility of it was horrendous to contemplate! Which was the reason she had turned down his invitation to see her again, and also the reason why she had left so abruptly on Sunday evening.

But the knowledge that she dared not go out with Jonas again, because of her past involvement with Ben, was hurting her so deeply she didn't know what to do about it. Or if she could do anything…!

'Jonas…' Harrie repeated appreciatively. 'That's a strong-sounding name.'

Jonas was strong. He was a dedicated and responsible doctor, too. Unfortunately, one of the other qualities Danie had admired in him, that of being a caring son and brother, precluded any further relationship between the two of them!

'So who is he?' Harried probed interestedly. 'And where did you meet him?'

Both questions Danie couldn't answer. Not without bringing Jonas's visit to their father on Saturday into the conversation, and she really didn't want to do that. Harrie had only been married a few weeks, she and Quinn obviously ecstatically happy together, and Danie did not want to be the one to burst that bubble of happiness by encouraging her older sister into helping her second-guess the reason why Jonas had attended their father. No doubt they would all be told in time.

But, in the meantime, Danie was stuck in a dilemma about Jonas. She longed to see him again, ached for him, but the part of her that had been so badly hurt by Ben in the past told her she would only be leaving herself open to further pain.

But she still *wanted* to see Jonas again!

'Where I met him isn't important.' She pretended disinterest. 'Neither is who he is,' she added firmly.

Harrie shook her head. 'Then what's the problem? Is it a one-sided attraction—is that it?' Although her tone of voice seemed to imply that was something she just didn't believe.

Danie felt grateful for her sister's confidence in her ability to be attractive to men, but at the same time she knew that wasn't the issue. 'Not exactly,' she hedged.

'But there is a problem?' Harrie pressed.

Danie wished she had never started this! But she also knew it was too late to stop now. Her sister could be tenacious when she chose, and she was obviously intrigued by this situation.

Danie drew in a deep breath. 'Harrie, he's Ben's ex-brother-in-law!' she burst out. And then stared wide-eyed at her sister as she waited for her reaction.

Harrie opened her mouth to speak. And then closed it again. Opened her mouth. And then closed it again.

Danie couldn't help it—she laughed. 'This has to be a first. I've certainly never seen a speechless Harrie before!'

'I—I just—' Harrie shook her head dazedly. 'How do you do it, Danie?' She pulled a face. 'Of all the men—'

'In all the world, he had to walk into my life,' Danie finished in a not-bad imitation of Humphrey Bogart, even if the quote was completely incorrect. 'And to answer your question, Harrie; I have no idea.' She sighed. 'He was just there. And—and he's gorgeous. And when he kissed me it was like—'

'It's gone as far as him kissing you?' Harrie squeaked. 'Just how long have you been keeping him a secret?'

It seemed as if she had always known Jonas, but she knew that in reality it was only a matter of days. Harrie simply wouldn't understand her problem if she told her that, would tell her to just cut her losses and move on. But, unlike with Ben, where Jonas was concerned that was something she didn't feel able to do.

'That isn't important,' Danie said impatiently. 'What is

important is the fact that Jonas's sister was married to Ben when I was going out with him. I'm probably the reason his sister divorced her husband!' she added emotionally.

'Now you don't know that—'

'Does it matter?' Danie interrupted heatedly. 'I met Nikki. Only briefly, granted, but I could see by the look on her face that she knew I was involved with Ben. She isn't likely to have forgotten me, Harrie!' She winced.

And Jonas, once he knew she had been involved with a married man—even if it were unwittingly!—with his own brother-in-law, simply wouldn't want to know her!

There just didn't seem to be a way forward for Jonas and her!

Harrie drew in a deep breath. 'It is a little complicated, I grant you—'

'Thanks!' Danie returned.

Harrie mock-glared at her. 'But not unsolvable, surely? If he doesn't already know, have you thought of simply telling Jonas the truth?'

Danie had thought of nothing else since Sunday! But she knew that, once she had done that, there would be no possibility of seeing Jonas again; his loyalty to his sister was a solid fact. As was his disgust with Ben. That disgust was sure to include any woman who had been involved with him...!

'He simply wouldn't understand, Harrie,' she persisted heavily.

Harrie pursed her lips thoughtfully. 'Are you sure you aren't underestimating him, Danie? Obviously I don't know Jonas, but anyone with a grain of sense would know that Ben was nothing but a charming rogue—'

'Thanks again!' Danie said. Her own common sense seemed to be something that had been distinctly lacking during her brief relationship with Ben.

'I didn't mean you,' her sister reproved. 'But you said there are children in the marriage—'

'Don't!' Danie cringed at the memory of discovering that not only was Ben married, but that he also had two children, innocents, who certainly didn't deserve to have the feckless Ben as their father.

'You're missing my point, Danie,' her sister continued. 'If there are children, then Ben had been married to Nikki for some years—certainly long enough, probably, for your Jonas to have realised Ben wasn't exactly faithful to his wife!'

'Maybe. But then again, maybe not...' Danie shrugged. 'And he isn't *my* Jonas,' she corrected.

'But you would like him to be,' Harrie guessed. 'Now come on, Danie; where's the determined sister I know and love? Because I can tell you now, *that* Danie wouldn't let a little thing like Ben Trainer keep her from the man she had set her heart on!'

Harrie was right, Danie knew she was. It was just that, after two years of refusing to get involved with any man, these feelings she had discovered she had for Jonas were unsettling enough, without the realisation that he was the ex-brother-in-law of the man who had caused her to be so wary of involvement in the first place!

It didn't seem to matter from which direction she approached the problem, she always came back to the fact that Nikki Trainer was Jonas's sister...!

'When are you seeing Jonas again?' Harrie asked thoughtfully.

Danie drew in a ragged breath. 'I'm not.'

'Not? But—' Harrie broke off as the waiter came to take their food order.

But it turned out that neither woman was particularly

interested in food any more, each ordering only a Caesar salad.

'Why aren't you seeing Jonas again?' Harrie demanded to know as soon as the two of them were alone again.

'I've just told you—'

'Forget about Ben for the moment—'

'I can't!' Danie groaned. 'Do you think Jonas has forgotten about him? About the way Ben betrayed his sister? With me!' she added forcefully.

'Do you want to know what I really think, Danie...?' her sister replied.

'I wouldn't have asked if I didn't!' she came back tautly.

Harrie nodded. 'Oh, I think you would. What you really want me to do, Danie, is agree with everything you've said, condone your decision not to see Jonas again. And you know something? I'm not going to do it. The last thing I've ever thought you were was a coward, Danie—'

'Because I'm not!' Danie's eyes flashed deeply green in warning.

'Then stop acting like one.' Harrie gave her hand a reassuring squeeze to take the sting out of her words. 'If you remember, things weren't exactly smooth-running for Quinn and myself at first,' she reminded her sister wryly. 'And look how marvellously that's turned out.'

'That's different—'

'No, it isn't,' Harrie told her. 'Give Jonas a call and invite him out to dinner.'

Danie hesitated. 'I did the inviting last time.'

'You—? No, don't tell me.' Harrie raised her hands in frustration. 'The only advice I can give you, Danie,' she said as the waiter approached the table with their salads, 'is not to run away from this, but face it head-on. It's the way you usually approach everything else!' she reminded her affectionately.

Harrie was right. This wasn't like her at all. She had never been one to run away from situations, good or bad. And during the last two years, since Ben's duplicity, that had been more than true of everything.

Was she behaving like a coward? Had Harrie been right when she'd guessed that Danie wanted her to tell her to cut her losses with Jonas and move on? Had she really become that frightened of emotional involvement...?

Besides, there was no guarantee that if she went out with Jonas again she wouldn't end up thinking all this soul-searching had been a complete waste of time, that she was only mildly infatuated, physically attracted rather than emotionally, after all.

Maybe she *would* give him a call...

'Danie?' Jonas didn't just sound surprised at the identity of his caller, he *was* surprised. *Very.* Danie had made it more than clear on Sunday night that she didn't intend seeing him again, cuttingly so, as he remembered.

Which was why, when Dorothy had buzzed through to him a few minutes ago to tell him there was a Miss Summer on the line for him, Danie had been the last Summer sister he had imagined to hear!

'The one and only,' her voice came back brittlely down the telephone line. 'I acquired your telephone number from my father; I hope you don't mind?'

Jonas didn't mind at all, but he couldn't help wondering what Rome Summer had made of the request! 'What can I do for you, Danie?' he said briskly.

There didn't sound as if there were any guns blazing, but with Danie, he was quickly learning, you never could tell!

'I've decided to accept your dinner invitation, after all,' she informed him lightly.

It didn't need two guesses why, Jonas realised ruefully; Danie was obviously *still* looking for information concerning his visit to her father's home last Saturday!

'If it's still open, of course,' she ventured at his prolonged silence.

Was it still open? Part of him knew that the last thing he should be doing was deepening his acquaintance with Danie Summer, but the other part of him, the part that remembered their response to each other, gave him a completely different answer...

'It's still open, Danie,' he assured her.

'Which evening would suit you?' she asked briskly.

Tonight. Tomorrow. The evening after. Any evening, he knew, would suit him for seeing Danie again.

Then common sense kicked in. Danie wasn't really interested in him, was the relative of a patient of his, and was really only after information. Whereas he...

'Are you sure, in the circumstances, that this is a good idea, Danie?' he questioned.

'Frightened, Jonas?' she came back tauntingly.

Of falling for a woman who obviously felt nothing towards him but a casual sense of amusement while she tried to prise information out of him? Of falling for Danie Summer at all?

Hell, *yes*, he was frightened!

'I'll even cook dinner for us at my apartment, Jonas,' she broke into his jumbled thoughts. 'Amongst all those flying lessons I took in my late teens, I also spent a year in France learning how to cook. My father, practical soul that he is, thought I should have more than one string to my bow,' she explained dryly. 'I think the theory was that as well as flying all over the world, I would at least be able to feed the man in my life, when I *was* at home!'

That sounded like the Rome Summer he had come to

know over the last few days, Jonas thought. But how much more dangerous would it be—for him!—to eat alone with Danie at her apartment...?

'Tomorrow evening will be fine,' he heard himself accept tersely. 'Although I believe the suggestion was that I take you out to dinner?'

'Take a rain check,' Danie dismissed easily.

Nothing threw this woman, Jonas acknowledged. She was completely in control, of herself, and every situation that was thrown at her.

Once again Jonas had the feeling of getting involved when he would be wiser not to...!

But wasn't it too late for that? Even if he turned down this idea of dinner together, the two of them would still see each other again. And the last two sleepless nights told him that he didn't need to see Danie to think about her until sleep became impossible!

'Okay, Danie, dinner at your apartment it is,' he accepted decisively. 'But I'll bring the wine.'

'You don't know what we'll be eating,' she said.

'Then I'll bring a bottle of red and white so that I cover all contingencies,' Jonas rejoined. 'Now I'm rather busy at the moment, so if you would just give me your address, we can continue this tomorrow evening.'

Not the best of ways to end the conversation, he decided a few seconds later once the call had been terminated by a seemingly cheery, undampened Danie.

Damn it, he had decided, during the last two days, that he would be a fool if he saw Danie on a social basis again. One telephone call from her and those well-intentioned decisions had flown straight out of the window!

Damn, damn, damn!

'Jonas, I wondered if you could just— What's wrong with you?' Dorothy, his middle-aged assistant and secretary of many years, had come to an abrupt halt in the doorway, looking across at him now with questioningly raised auburn brows.

Come to think of it, Dorothy was a redhead, too, Jonas realised as he looked at her properly for the first time in years. He was starting to feel that they had him surrounded!

'Nothing,' he snapped. 'What do you have there?' He indicated the papers she held in her hand.

'Just some letters for you to sign,' she replied distractedly, still studying him thoughtfully. 'Your call from Miss Summer seems to have—disturbed you?'

Jonas glared at his secretary across the width of the room. 'My mood has nothing to do with the call from Miss Summer,' he informed her.

'Oh.' Dorothy nodded slowly. 'But you accept you are in a mood? In fact,' she added before he could make a reply, 'you've been like a bear with a sore head all week.'

'It's only Tuesday!' Jonas came back tersely.

'Quite long enough to put up with your snappiness,' Dorothy informed him as she crossed the room to place the letters on the desk in front of him.

'Dorothy—'

'Yes, Jonas?' she answered innocently.

He let out a deflated sigh. What was the point? Dorothy ran his practice with the ease of an efficient sergeant major, always polite but necessarily firm with his patients, while at the same time safeguarding his privacy. He was in no position to complain if that allowed her a lot of leeway where the two of them were concerned. Besides, Dorothy knew him too well to be fobbed off by any cutting remarks on his part!

He gave a half-smile. 'I'm sorry if I've been less than—

cheerful, the last day or so,' he apologised. 'I have a lot on my mind at the moment.'

'Miss Summer, for example,' Dorothy put in knowingly.

'Her name's Danie, Dorothy,' he put in heavily, knowing Dorothy wouldn't be satisfied until she knew at least that about the other woman.

'Danie?' Dorothy frowned. 'But I thought—'

'Never mind what you thought, Dorothy.' He sighed. 'There are three Summer sisters: Harriet, Danielle, and Andrea. And not necessarily in that order.'

Dorothy gave an amused smile. 'Bit of a handful, is she?'

His mouth twisted ruefully. 'Something like that. Now could we get back to work, do you think?' he continued briskly. 'Danie Summer has taken up enough of my time for one afternoon!'

Dorothy gave him another knowing look before turning on her heel and leaving the room.

Jonas relaxed back in his high-backed leather chair for the first time since he had answered the telephone several minutes ago and had stiffened in recognition at the sound of Danie's voice.

Strangely enough, although he had no idea where this was going to take him—if he did know he would probably start running now and not stop!—he felt more relaxed than he had since Sunday.

And he knew the reason for that was that he was going to spend tomorrow evening with Danie...

Danie of the sharp tongue. Danie the derider. Danie of the flaming red hair... Danie of the beautiful green eyes... Danie of the kissable mouth...!

She was heaven and hell, Jonas decided affectionately.

But she was also the only woman he wanted to spend time with.

Well...tomorrow evening, at least!

CHAPTER SIX

PERFECT, Danie decided as she looked at the dinner table she had prepared for Jonas and herself. It was a round table, and as such the two of them should have been able to sit opposite each other. But Danie had chosen to seat them next to each other on the curve.

Much friendlier, she acknowledged with satisfaction. Friendly...? Was that what she now wanted to be with Jonas?

All her father's remarks about the contrariness of women came flooding back. But Danie didn't consider she was being contrary; she had just been kissed by the man who had seemed to be the other half of herself!

Their bodies, at least, had seemed to recognise each other on Sunday night, even if, at twenty-seven and thirty-eight respectively, their hearts were a little more jaundiced than that. And if Danie hadn't spotted that photograph of a relaxed and smiling Ben, standing beside his wife—Jonas's sister!—and two daughters, heaven knew what would have happened!

But it was what was going to happen tonight that filled her thoughts now!

She had tried to think of something about Jonas that she disliked—but the truth was, she just couldn't find a thing. He was attractive, charming, obviously successful, and he appeared to have the same family values that she did. Even that habit he had—annoying though it was!—of sidestepping her questions concerning her father's health was merely another indication of his professional integrity.

But there must be something; it simply wasn't possible to fall in love with someone on a few days' acquaintance— was it...? Tonight would give her the answer to that. It must!

The table looked great, the food was ready for cooking in the kitchen, so now she could concentrate on her own appearance. On Sunday she had deliberately dressed to attract; tonight, in her own apartment, she would wear something a little less dazzling.

The simple black knee-length dress that she finally decided upon—half a dozen other dresses lay on the bed, considered and discarded—was certainly that, but it nevertheless showed the slender perfection of her body, her hair a scarlet flame against its darkness, green eyes huge, if a little wary, in the creamy beauty of her face.

Jonas, when she opened the apartment door a few minutes later in answer to the ring of the bell, seemed to have had a similar problem as to how he should dress for the evening, although his choice of cream shirt, teamed with brown trousers and a casually fitting brown jumper, certainly took Danie's breath away. As did the bunch of yellow roses he held in his hand.

He grinned as he saw her wide-eyed gaze on the flowers. 'It was instilled in me at an early age that it's polite to arrive with a suitable gift for my hostess,' he said, holding out the roses towards Danie, maintaining his hold on the two bottles of wine he also carried, one red, and one white, as he had promised...

He couldn't have known—of course he couldn't!—but yellow roses were her favourite! Her mother had always grown roses, all the year round, in the hothouse Danie's father had built especially for her. Danie had spent hours herself in that hothouse as she'd followed her mother around. But the yellow roses, deep, almost gold, had always been Danie's favourite...

'You can take them, Danie,' Jonas teased softly as she stared at the roses. 'They aren't going to bite!'

As he'd said, they were a gesture of politeness from a guest to his hostess, nothing more. 'Thank you,' she accepted. 'Oh...!' she gasped as she took the blooms into her own arms, their heady perfume bringing into play aching nostalgia.

'What is it?' Jonas asked concernedly.

Snap out of it, Danie, she instructed herself firmly; otherwise Jonas was going to regret ever having accepted her invitation!

'Nothing.' She smiled brightly, opening the door wider for him to come in. 'Help yourself to some wine.' She indicated the tray on the side-dresser, the bottle of white wine already uncorked. 'I'll just go and do something with these.' She almost ran from the room with the roses in her arms.

She wasn't being exactly hospitable, Danie realised as she filled a vase up with water and dumped the roses unceremoniously into it. Yellow roses! Jonas couldn't have chosen to give her anything more disconcerting, her head now filled with memories of those happy hours she had spent with her mother amongst her own roses. But Jonas couldn't have known that, she chided herself, and there was no reason why he should guess now, either. As long as she pulled herself together and stopped behaving like an idiot!

'Oh, good.' She smiled brightly as she returned to the lounge and found Jonas seated in one of the armchairs, a glass of white wine dangling from his fingers.

'I poured one for you too.' Jonas nodded in the direction of the second glass as it stood on the dresser next to the

two bottles of wine he had brought himself. 'Are you sure
you're preparing dinner in there?' he teased, nodding in
the direction of the kitchen. 'I can't smell any food cooking.'

Danie gave him a sidelong glance. 'I have the feeling,
Mr Noble, that you may doubt my previous claims to cu-
linary greatness.'

Jonas grinned. 'Well…'

'Agas don't give off cooking smells,' she assured him,
picking up her own glass of wine and taking a sip.

His eyes widened. 'You really do cook!' he exclaimed
appreciatively. 'My mother says only serious cooks have
an Aga nowadays.'

'She's right,' Danie agreed.

'And here I've been imagining an army of caterers de-
livering trays of pre-prepared food, with strict instructions
to be away from here before I arrived at seven-thirty!'
Jonas mocked.

'Dream on,' Danie said with satisfaction, knowing that
the mushroom soufflé, followed by Dover sole and summer
vegetables, were going to be a success, and as for dessert—! Strawberry meringue, followed by a selection of
cheeses, couldn't be faulted, either.

'I can hardly wait,' Jonas murmured, looking at her between narrowed lids.

Danie gave him an assessing look, wondering what he
couldn't wait for. After all, they had been discussing dinner. At least, she thought they had…

'I'll just go and check on our first course,' she announced, before hurrying back into the kitchen, heaving a
deep sigh of relief once in there.

She was, she decided breathlessly, sadly out of practice
with the art of flirtation! If she had ever been in practice.
Harrie was right: Danie's approach had always been forth-

right and to the point. But somehow, with Jonas, that didn't seem the way to go. She—

'Problems?' Jonas queried as he followed her into the kitchen, standing mere feet away from her.

Only with her equilibrium. It just wasn't decent to want to forget all about dinner, and instead rip this man's clothes off, quickly followed by her own, before the two of them became nakedly entangled in the pleasure of lovemaking!

She swallowed hard. 'On the contrary,' she assured him in a slightly higher pitched tone than was natural to her. 'I was just about to serve our starter.' She moved away from him towards the Aga, instantly feeling a lessening of that magnetism that seemed to surround her when Jonas was too close to her.

So much for the hope that she would discover, on seeing Jonas again, that she had been imagining that physical attraction between them! If anything, it was more intense tonight than it had been on Sunday. Almost as if no time had elapsed at all and they were continuing where they had left off...!

She looked up sharply as Jonas made no move to leave the kitchen but instead stood watching her as she arranged the miniature soufflés on the already prepared plates. 'I'll bring these through in a moment,' she told him as she straightened.

'I'm fine where I am, thanks.' And as if to prove the point, he leant back against one of the kitchen units, taking a leisurely sip of his wine. 'Actually, to be completely honest,' he continued, 'I'm enjoying the sight of all this domesticity on your part—I never would have believed it of the tough lady pilot in the baseball cap and combat trousers that I met on Saturday!'

Danie felt the angry flush that darkened her cheeks. 'Then let's hope you aren't disappointed,' she snapped.

'What's the saying? "The proof of the pudding is in the eating"?' She picked up the two plates and swept past him out of the kitchen and into the dining-room.

This time the reason for her racing pulse wasn't Jonas's close proximity but pure annoyance. Damn the man! Being a pilot didn't mean she was bereft of feminine traits. Besides, as he was now going to discover, she was a very good cook.

She wished now she hadn't put their place settings quite so close together at the table, but as Jonas quietly entered the room behind her she knew it was too late to do anything about it, so she indicated his seat to the left of her.

'This is a nice big apartment,' Jonas murmured as he sat down.

'I pay the rent myself,' she said heatedly as she sat next to him, that angry flush still in her cheeks.

Jonas raised dark brows. 'I was merely commenting on the size of the apartment, Danie; I wasn't suggesting anything else,' he returned levelly, picking up his fork to eat the soufflé.

Danie cooled down a little. 'Most people, given my family background, seem to think I only play at working.'

Jonas looked at her with steady brown eyes. 'I don't believe you play at anything, Danie. And I'm not "most people",' he added huskily.

She swallowed hard, completely aware of the truth of that statement! Jonas was totally unlike any other man she had ever met.

'Eat your food,' she instructed abruptly.

'Yes, ma'am,' he responded in an amused voice, suiting his actions to his words. 'My God...!' he said after his first mouthful. 'If you ever get tired of flying, Danie, I suggest you open up a restaurant!' He told her this with genuine appreciation.

She smiled her own pleasure at the compliment. 'I'll never tire of flying, Jonas.' She laughed softly as she shook her head.

He paused in his eating, his gaze intense now. 'You changed your mind about seeing me again,' he reminded gruffly.

Danie turned away from his searching gaze. 'I thought that was a woman's prerogative,' she answered—which was no answer at all! But she didn't want to get into a conversation about why she had changed her mind!

Jonas's mouth curved upwards. 'I'll grant you, you're much more unpredictable than most!'

She turned back to look at him. 'And have there been a lot of women in your life, Jonas?' She had tried to sound lightly interested—but was fully aware that she had sounded anything but.

'Some.' He shrugged. 'Nothing serious, though. And you?'

She had known almost as soon as she'd put the question to him that it wasn't a subject she wished to be pursued concerning her own life—not when her own last serious relationship had been with this man's own married brother-in-law!

She moistened dry lips. 'Nothing serious,' she echoed his words, relieved to see Jonas had almost finished his soufflé. A few minutes' respite in the kitchen wouldn't come amiss right now!

'Which just leaves unattached you and me,' he said as he looked at her thoughtfully. 'Do you think this relationship is going anywhere?'

Danie drew in a sharp breath, attempting to make a reply—and failing!—then swallowing hard before trying again. 'I thought I was supposed to be the blunt one?' she finally managed to gasp, her appetite having now disappeared completely. 'Besides, we don't have a—a "relationship"!'

'Dinner together twice in a week seems to imply something,' he corrected softly.

She pushed her chair back noisily as she stood up to remove their plates. 'It means we both have to eat!' she said restlessly.

Jonas smiled as he turned to look up at her. 'That's a good answer, Danie—if completely inadequate for the question asked.' He sobered. 'And it wasn't an idle question, Danie; I do have a good reason for asking.'

She frowned down at him. 'I can't imagine what that could be,' she said tersely. 'What happened to letting things run their course?'

Jonas shrugged broad shoulders. 'Ordinarily that would be the best thing...' he granted slowly.

'But?'

'But in our case there are—complications,' he pointed out.

Danie stiffened, eyeing him warily, her hands tightly gripping the plates she held, her cheeks pale now.

Did Jonas already know? Had he somehow found out about her brief relationship with his brother-in-law? But if—

'I was talking about my professional relationship with a member of your family,' Jonas went on slowly, watching her intently. 'Danie, what—?'

Her light, dismissive laughter cut across whatever he had been going to say next, because she had a feeling it wasn't something she wanted to hear—or answer! 'I'm sure we're both adult enough to be able to deal with that situation,' she dismissed. 'If it becomes necessary. Now, you'll have to excuse me for a few minutes, Jonas,' she said quickly, 'or our next course will spoil.'

'Heaven forbid!'

Danie was aware of his appreciative gaze on her as she left the dining-room, only breathing more easily once the door had closed behind her.

Careful, Danie, she cautioned herself. She had almost jumped to a completely erroneous conclusion just then by assuming the complication Jonas referred to involved Ben. It was a conclusion she simply wasn't ready to deal with yet.

One thing she did know—she definitely was as attracted to Jonas as she had thought she had been on Sunday night...!

Jonas tried to remember what it was he had said that had caused Danie's defensive response seconds ago, shaking his head as the answer eluded him.

Of course, he had been being a bit forward in assuming they had, or indeed would have, a relationship, and yet somehow he knew that wasn't the reason Danie had suddenly become so wary.

He gave up trying to analyse the workings of Danie's mind. She was unlike any other woman he had ever met. In fact, she was completely unique. A tough, capable pilot at their first meeting, then a beautifully, totally feminine woman on Sunday evening, and now tonight—! Not only did she look good enough to eat, but she also cooked like a dream.

Jonas couldn't help wondering what other surprises were in store for him where Danie Summer was concerned!

The perfection of the rest of the meal she served them certainly came as no surprise to him; he was quickly learning that if Danie did something then she didn't just do it well, she did it superbly.

He found himself wondering, as the two of them lingered over their coffee and brandies back in the sitting-room, his offer to help clear away after their meal firmly refused, if Danie would make love as beautifully as she did everything else...

Relaxed by the good food, complementary wine, scintillating company, he looked across to the chair where she sat opposite him, with sleepily appreciative brown eyes.

Her hair was slightly tousled from the exertions of cooking, her face slightly flushed, that pouting mouth bare of lip-gloss after their meal; Danie looked warmly desirable. Jonas was quickly approaching the time when caution concerning this attraction flew out of the window. Actually, he had probably passed that from the moment he'd accepted her invitation to dine with her at her apartment!

'Is the brandy not to your liking?' Danie seemed to pick up on his now less-than-relaxed mood.

Her choice of brandy was as excellent as her good taste in everything else. It was his own good sense that he was starting to question...

'The brandy was perfect,' he assured her, putting the empty glass down before standing up to cross the room to where she sat, his eyes intense on the beauty of her flushed face as he pulled her effortlessly to her feet in front of him. 'In fact, Danie,' he continued, 'so far, this whole evening has been perfect.'

She seemed to swallow convulsively again as she looked up at him, her eyes shining like emeralds through those dark lashes. 'So far...?'

'Danie...!' he groaned throatily even as his head lowered and his mouth claimed hers.

This was what he had wanted from the moment she had opened the door to him two hours ago. And he hadn't been mistaken on Sunday; Danie's body *did* fit against his as if it formed the other half of himself!

God, she felt so good, her soft curves moulded to his harder ones, her arms about his neck as she met the passion of his kiss.

His hands cradled each side of her face as he sipped and tasted the nectar of her lips, swollen now in her arousal, those hands then becoming entangled in the fire of her hair as he pulled her harder against him.

Jonas had never felt the rightness of this before in all of his thirty-eight years, and right now he wanted Danie too much to feel in the least wary of such all-consuming desire.

Her breast felt firm but warmly arousing as one of his hands cupped that pouting curve through the silk of her dress, knowing in that moment that she wore no bra, the material merely a whisper of fabric between his hand and her warmth. But even that whisper was too much of a barrier, and he knew a longing to have a completely naked Danie curved into his own nakedness.

The zip of the dress slid smoothly down the length of her spine. The dress, once removed from her shoulders, slipped easily to the carpeted floor at their feet.

Her nipple was already aroused against his thumb-tip, and Jonas could feel the leap of his own body as he bent and took that second aroused pink nub into the warm cavern of his mouth, his tongue lapping the creamy warmth there as Danie held him gently against her.

She wore only silky black panties, he quickly discovered as he pulled her thighs against his own pulsing ones, and her skin was as smooth as his hands moved to cup her beneath the silky material and pull her closer to his hardness.

'Jonas…!' she groaned achingly.

He raised his head to look at her, recognising the reciprocal passion in those deep green eyes, her breath coming in short gasps, her hand trembling slightly as she entwined her fingers in the thick darkness of his hair.

Jonas looked at her slender loveliness, knowing that he wanted Danie more than he had ever wanted anything, or anyone, in his life before.

'Danie, I—' He broke off abruptly as a strange ringing noise broke through that sensual aura that had enclosed them both these last few minutes. 'What the hell...?' He looked frowningly around the room for the source of that ringing.

'Leave it, Jonas. It's only the telephone—and I don't want to talk to anyone just now!' Danie told him breathlessly as she pulled his head back down to hers, their lips once again fusing in that electric desire.

But the ringing noise persisted, so much so that after a minute or so Jonas couldn't stand it any more, let alone concentrate on making love to Danie, and raised his head once more to look for the telephone. Even if he could only take the receiver off the hook so that the caller couldn't telephone back!

'Whoever it is is very persistent.' He scowled his displeasure, holding Danie at arm's length now. 'If I answer that—' he nodded darkly in the direction of the telephone on the dresser next to the drinks tray '—it isn't going to be some disgruntled boyfriend on the other end of the line, is it?' Just the thought of it made him feel like strangling someone!

It took Danie some seconds to gather her passion-scattered wits together enough to realise what he had just said, but when she finally did she didn't look at all pleased by his remark. 'It won't be a boyfriend, disgruntled or otherwise—because I don't have one!' she assured him, stepping back into her dress to zip it back into place with the minimum of movement.

As if she had done it dozens of times before, Jonas decided resentfully.

Although the fact that she was now once again fully dressed couldn't take away the fact of her passion-swollen lips, or the desire that still shone in those dark green eyes!

'Hey, let's not argue about a telephone call, Danie,' Jonas cajoled as the ringing finally stopped without either of them having answered the call. 'I apologise for the unnecessary remark I made a few minutes ago. My only excuse is that, although I've had years of being trained to answer telephone calls—for obvious reasons!—I just wasn't expecting there to be one at this particular moment.' He self-deprecatingly explained the inner disappointment he felt that the call had obviously put an end to their passionate interlude.

Danie gave a pained sigh. 'I'm no more thrilled about it than you are. I—' She broke off with an angry frown as the telephone began to ring once again. 'Persistent is about right!' she muttered as she moved to snatch up the receiver—only to find that the ringing noise continued...! She looked across at Jonas with completely puzzled eyes.

But Jonas was no longer in the least puzzled. 'It's my mobile,' he acknowledged as he moved to pick up his cellular telephone from where he had placed it on a side table when Danie had gone to the kitchen to put the roses in water; he had forgotten all about the stupid thing in his enjoyment of the evening—especially the last few minutes of it!

'The price you pay for having all those private—and rich—patients,' Danie bit out caustically before turning away.

Damn, damn, damn, Jonas muttered angrily to himself as he realised he had once again taken one step forward with Danie—only to find himself instantly taking two steps back!

'Yes?' he answered tersely into the receiver of his mobile telephone, his anger turning to concern as he instantly recognised the voice of his caller. 'Nikki...?' he cut in gently on the slightly hysterical gabble on the other end of the line.

Even as he listened attentively to the voice of his sister he glanced across at Danie apologetically for the interruption, grimacing slightly as she indicated she was going into the kitchen.

The evening, Jonas guessed, was over as far as he and Danie were concerned.

Damn, damn, *damn*!

CHAPTER SEVEN

NIKKI!

There was no surer way to put a dampener on Danie's aroused emotions than the mention of Jonas's sister's name. An actual telephone call from her had the effect, as far as Danie was concerned, of finishing their evening together completely!

After making her excuses to Jonas, Danie walked steadily towards the kitchen, knowing that he continued to watch her every move even as he carried on the conversation with his sister. It was a conversation Danie did her best not to listen to; the less she knew about Nikki Trainer, the better it would be for all of them!

She leant shakily back against one of the kitchen units once the door had closed behind her, groaning into her hands as she realised exactly what Nikki would have been interrupting if that call had come even five minutes later than it had. As it was, it was going to be difficult to face Jonas again after the intimacies they had just shared.

Seconds ago she had been almost completely naked— while Jonas had remained fully clothed!

She loved the man!

Danie knew it as certainly as she knew she would draw her next breath. But Nikki Trainer's telephone call had been a timely reminder that her love for Jonas was at best a risk, and at worst a disaster. She—

'Sorry about that,' Jonas apologised as he joined her in the kitchen, his movements tense. 'That was my sister,' he explained unnecessarily.

100

Danie had dropped her hands down from in front of her face as soon as he'd entered the room, straightening away from the kitchen unit now; the last thing she wanted was for him to see just how affected she had been by the passion they had just shared.

'Everything okay?' she asked, knowing by the grimness of his expression that it wasn't. Besides, it was ten-thirty at night; not too many people, even sisters, telephoned for a casual chat at that time of night!

Jonas shook his head. 'It's my niece's birthday today. She's eight. Nikki had a birthday party for her earlier. Which is the reason I'm dressed so casually, by the way. I called in to the party with Suzie's present on my way here.'

'That was nice,' Danie returned tightly—knowing he hadn't got to the problem yet…

'It was, actually,' he came back hardly. 'But apparently, shortly after I left there, Suzie's father arrived, on the same pretext.'

Ben!

Danie stiffened warily. 'I take it Nikki is the sister who's divorced?' Even as she asked the question Danie knew she was digging herself into a hole she might have trouble getting herself out of.

She *knew* Nikki was his divorced sister, knew the reason for Nikki's divorce too—she ought to!—and by pretending anything else she was putting herself into an untenable position.

'She is,' Jonas acknowledged heavily. 'And having arrived at Nikki's home with a present for Suzie, Ben is now proving very difficult to get rid of. In fact,' he bit out tersely, 'he's refusing to go at all! He was always a bit of a bully where Nik and the children were concerned, liked his own way all the time, and poor Nik was always a bit scared of his temper. She only managed to escape to telephone me now with the excuse she was going upstairs to check on the children.'

'I see,' Danie said slowly. This behaviour didn't sound like the Ben she had known at all; in retrospect, she had decided he was far too self-centred to be interested in anyone but himself! But perhaps it would be a different matter if that self-interest were challenged...?

Jonas watched her carefully. 'I hope you do—because Nikki has asked me to go over there to help get rid of him.'

Danie met his eyes. 'So what's keeping you?'

'You are,' he told her softly, reaching out to lightly grasp the tops of her arms. 'You invited me here for the evening, and it seems very rude to just eat and run.'

Danie felt the colour enter her cheeks as she easily recalled he had done far more than that, her eyes dropping away from his now. 'If it was one of my sisters who had telephoned me for help, I would be doing exactly the same as you are,' she assured him bluntly.

Jonas chuckled softly, pulling her gently into his arms, her head now resting against his shoulder. 'I was hoping you would say that!' He sighed his relief at her reaction to his predicament.

Danie raised her head to look up at him. 'Your ex-brother-in-law isn't likely to turn nasty, is he?' Ben had always struck her as being too lazy to rouse himself to physical violence, but refusing to leave his ex-wife's home seemed out of character for the man she had known too...

Jonas shrugged. 'I have no idea. But he's upsetting Nikki—and that I won't have. She's already suffered enough on his account.'

Danie extricated herself from Jonas's arms as she stepped back from him, avoiding looking at him, aware that she was one of the reasons Nikki had suffered! 'I really think you had better go,' she told him tonelessly.

Jonas looked at her with puzzlement. 'Can I call you later? Just to let you know I haven't been beaten to a pulp!'

She smiled at his attempt to joke, although she was inwardly pleased at his suggestion that he call her. This evening had come to rather an abrupt end, and her emotions were feeling a little raw. 'Please do.' She turned to find a piece of paper in one of the drawers, writing down her telephone number before handing it to him.

He slipped the paper into his shirt pocket. 'There's more than a little subterfuge to my request,' he admitted. 'This way I'll also be able to invite you out to dinner when I call!'

Danie gave a wry smile. 'That will be a novelty!' After all, so far she had done all the inviting! Well...except for that one dinner invitation Jonas had made—and which she had promptly turned down!

He laughed, before sobering at the lack of humour on her own pale face. 'Are you sure you're all right with this?' he questioned. 'Because if it bothers you—'

'It doesn't bother me. Now go!' And to suit her actions to her words she grasped him firmly by the shoulders and turned him in the direction of the door. 'Your poor sister is probably at screaming pitch by now if Ben is proving as difficult to remove as you said.'

'Hmm!' he replied. 'I don't know why the wretched man can't just leave her alone.' They walked towards the door. 'He had his chance, and he blew it, big time—'

'Maybe he's a man who just doesn't like to lose,' Danie suggested distractedly—the last thing she wanted was to hear exactly how Ben had blown his marriage to Jonas's sister!

'Maybe.' Jonas scowled. 'But Nikki has just started to

get her life back in order, has been going out with someone else for the last couple of months—'

'Well, there you have your answer as to why Ben's behaving this way,' Danie cut in knowingly, choosing her next words carefully. 'This Ben probably thought your sister would go on grieving for her lost marriage for ever,' she explained. 'Besides, it's a well-known fact that finding out an ex-partner has someone else in their life is a sure-fire reason for the ex-husband, or wife, wanting to come back.'

Jonas stared down at her as he stood beside the door. 'You seem very knowledgeable about these things...?'

'Not from personal experience, I can assure you,' she told him with a short laugh. 'Just a casual observance of human nature,' she assured him.

'Whatever,' Jonas accepted. 'Ben certainly isn't going to mess Nikki's life up a second time.'

Danie smiled at his determination, sure that Jonas was more than capable of handling his ex-brother-in-law. 'Go get him,' she encouraged—after all, she had no reason to feel in the least kindly towards Ben herself!

Jonas bent and lightly kissed her on the lips. 'I'll call you later,' he promised.

Danie's legs were shaking so badly by the time Jonas left that she had to stagger back into the sitting-room and sit down—before she fell down!

Well, she had more than answered her own questions where Jonas was concerned. She was in love with him. And the fact that Nikki Trainer was his sister was going to be as destructive to that love as Danie had feared it might be.

Jonas obviously cared very deeply for his sister, and his loyalty, if brought into question, would lie with Nikki.

Which left Danie where...?

*   *   *

Jonas's expression was grim as he faced his ex-brother-in-law across the sitting-room of his sister's home half an hour later. Ben was proving as much of an idiot as he had always been, claiming he had a right to visit his own children. The fact that those children had been in bed for the last two hours of this so-called visit seemed to have escaped him completely!

'Besides, Nikki invited me to stay for coffee,' Ben announced triumphantly.

Jonas's mouth tightened, and he didn't even glance in the direction of his pale-faced sister, his attention all focused on the petulant good looks of his dark-haired ex-brother-in-law. 'Nikki has always been polite—even to people who don't deserve such good manners!'

Ben's mouth twisted; he was confidently relaxed as he lounged back in one of the armchairs. 'I still don't understand what you're doing back here, Jonas; you've already delivered Suzie's birthday present, and Nikki and I were just sitting here talking over old times.'

Now Jonas did spare his sister a glance, knowing by the pale delicacy of her cheeks that this trip down Memory Lane had not been a pleasant experience for her. Of course it hadn't, damn it; she had once loved this man to distraction, and he had betrayed that love in the cruellest way possible.

His mouth tightened even more as he turned back to Ben. 'You've talked them over, Ben—now I suggest you leave!'

The other man raised dark brows. 'And if I choose not to do so?'

'Then I suppose I'll have to make you,' Jonas returned mildly.

Ben sat forward, his eyes narrowing angrily now. 'You always were an interfering bast—'

'And you were never good enough to even clean my sister's shoes, let alone marry her!' Jonas cut in harshly on the expletive, his hands clenched into knuckle-white fists at his sides as he scowled down at the other man.

Ben gave a humourless smile. 'You never did think I was good enough for her.'

'And I was right.' Jonas bit out disgustedly. 'Now are you going to leave peacefully—or do I have to involve the police in this?' He heard Nikki's gasp of protest at such a suggestion, but continued to meet the other man's stare challengingly. Ben might be able to bully a defenceless woman, a woman who had once loved him, but Jonas didn't have such emotions to cloud his own judgement. He was determined that Ben would leave, one way or another...!

Ben shook his head confidently. 'I very much doubt you want it to come to that any more than I do,' he drawled. 'Jonas Noble, the doctor darling of society, the—'

'That's enough, Ben.' Nikki was the one to cut in this time, her voice shaking slightly in her agitation. 'You can upset me all you like, but I won't have you being rude to my brother—'

'Of course not,' Ben acknowledged mockingly, shaking his head as he finally stood up. 'It was the biggest mistake of my life when I became involved with this family!' His eyes raked scathingly over his ex-wife. 'I can't understand what this new man in your life sees in you, Nikki; you've certainly let yourself go the last couple of years.'

Jonas felt the red tide of anger well up inside him at this deliberate hurting of a woman who had already suffered enough at this man's hands. 'Why, you—'

'Just go, Ben,' Nikki interrupted evenly, Jonas feeling proud of her as her head went back challengingly. 'And don't come back here again.'

Ben appeared unperturbed. 'The last I heard I still had reasonable access to my own two children—'

'You still do,' Nikki stated. 'But after this little fiasco I will drop the children off to you in future.' She looked at him with distaste. 'You'll just have to make sure your lady-friend has vacated your apartment before I do—otherwise the children won't be stopping!'

Ben's eyes were glacial now. 'I'll do what I please—'

'Not with my children, you won't,' Nikki told him hardly. 'I don't want any of your women near them. I don't suppose it's still the same woman?'

Ben's eyes narrowed. 'You assume correctly.'

Nikki snorted. 'She looked too good for you, Ben, very beautiful too; it's good to know she had enough sense to dump you!'

'I said *I* stopped seeing her, Nikki,' Ben retorted. 'I could have her back in my life like that—' he gave a snap of his fingers '—if I wanted to.'

'Then more fool her,' Nikki returned calmly.

For all her distaste for her ex-husband, Jonas could nonetheless see that his sister was getting close to breaking-point. Which, in the circumstances, wasn't surprising!

Ben's affairs, once realised by Nikki, had been the final ending of a marriage that had been rocky for some time. Why, Ben had even introduced his wife to one of them!

'The two of you probably deserve each other,' Jonas told the other man disgustedly. 'Now I repeat, Ben, are you going to leave, or does force have to be used?'

'Oh, don't worry, I'm going,' Ben sneered with a hard, humourless laugh. 'I find all this righteous indignation as nauseating as I did two years ago!' He strode angrily to the door. 'And maybe I should give Danie a call; at least she knows how to have a good time!' came his parting shot.

The front door of the house slammed shut behind him seconds later, but Jonas, for one, was unaware of it.

Danie!

Ben had said he would give *Danie* a call!

No, it couldn't be the same Danie. Not *his* Danie.

But she wasn't his. Admittedly, they had come pretty close to it this evening, but Nikki's telephone call had interrupted them.

Danie…?

It couldn't be the same Danie!

Could it…?

'Here.' Nikki held out a glass of brandy to him, a second one for herself in her other hand. 'After that I think we both need it!' she said with relief.

Jonas took a gulp of the fiery liquid, not even noticing as it burnt a trail down the back of his throat. It couldn't be his Danie!

Nikki sat down gratefully in one of the armchairs, sipping her own brandy. 'Every time I begin to wonder if I could have been wrong about Ben he proves to me all over again that I wasn't.' She glanced up at Jonas as she received no response. 'I'm really sorry about disturbing you this evening, Jonas,' she said. 'I just didn't want to involve Graham in this.'

Jonas could understand her not wanting to complicate matters by bringing her partner into what was already a difficult situation. 'It's okay,' he said quietly, still preoccupied with thoughts of Danie. The possibility of Danie and Ben…?

Nikki looked at him carefully. 'Did I interrupt something important when I called you earlier?'

He had thought his relationship with Danie was important. Now he wasn't so sure.

But Danie wasn't such an unusual name. It didn't have

to be the same Danie. Danie could be the diminutive of several female names, it didn't have to be the shortened version of Danielle.

All he had to do was ask Nikki for a description of this particular Danie—

No, he couldn't do that!

Because part of him didn't want to know...?

Part of him feared knowing...!

Because if Nikki's description of the other woman should confirm that it was Danie Summer they were all talking about, then Danie must have known earlier exactly who he'd been talking about, when he'd discussed Nikki and Ben!

Did he really believe that the forthright Danie he knew could be *that* underhand?

No, of course she couldn't. Danie had been blunt to the point of rudeness from the first moment he'd met her. There was no way, absolutely no way, he could ever believe she had been involved with a married man, that her relationship with him had eventually broken up the marriage.

That decided to his satisfaction, Jonas turned his attention back to Nikki. 'You did interrupt something,' he admitted with a relaxed smile. 'But luckily it was with an understanding woman.'

Nikki's eyes sparkled interestedly. 'You didn't tell me you were seeing someone, Jonas,' she reproved affectionately.

'I don't know that I am—yet,' he replied enigmatically. 'But if and when I am, you'll be the first to know,' he promised.

'Good enough,' his sister accepted, knowing better than to push the subject; she probably knew from experience that Jonas could be extremely tight-lipped when it came to his own private life. 'Goodness, I hope I never have a repeat of this evening.' She shuddered delicately. 'It seems to be my relationship with Graham that has set Ben off.'

'I've been told that often happens when an ex-partner learns you're involved with someone else.' Jonas heard himself repeating Danie's earlier words.

Nikki raised blonde brows; she was still prettily attractive at forty-one—despite what Ben had said to the contrary earlier! 'And who told you that?' she teased, obviously relieved the encounter with Ben was at an end.

Jonas grinned. 'Never mind.' He sobered. 'Now are you going to be all right, or do you want me to stay the night in case Ben decides to come back?'

His sister shook her head. 'He probably thinks that's exactly what you're going to do, so I'm sure he won't come back tonight,' Nikki said with certainty. 'Besides, he was going off to telephone this woman, Danie, remember?'

Oh, Jonas remembered all right. But it wasn't his Danie, because he was going to telephone her himself as soon as he reached home.

Danie Summer having the same first name as the woman who had wrecked his sister's marriage could prove a little complicated if his own relationship with her flourished, but that was something he would have to deal with if and when. At the moment, there were more immediate things to be done.

'You know,' his sister continued, 'if I ever see that particular young woman again, I think I may just thank her... For being instrumental in helping me make the decision to end years of hell!'

Jonas put down his own empty brandy glass. 'Don't let anything Ben said just now bother you, Nik,' he advised as he bent to kiss her on the cheek. 'It was only sour grapes on his part; anyone can see you're as lovely as ever,' he assured her. 'More so, actually,' he added as he studied her thoughtfully. 'Could it be that my little sister is in love?'

Nikki's cheeks flushed fiery-red. 'Less of the little, Buster; I'll always be three years older than you!'

'Well, that neatly avoided giving me an answer,' Jonas murmured appreciatively.

His sister's mouth quirked ruefully. 'Wait and see,' she said enigmatically. 'Dorothy approves, anyway.'

'Dorothy?' Jonas echoed, brows raised. 'My Dorothy?'

'I'm sure she would love to hear you call her that!' Nikki chuckled. 'She babysits for me sometimes so that Graham and I can go out,' she explained at his perplexed expression.

'She never mentioned it. And neither did you until just now...' Jonas felt dazed. 'You know, I think Ben may have just underestimated you, Nikki...'

His sister smiled. 'For the last time,' she said, standing up. 'I really am grateful to you for helping me tonight, Jonas—especially as I seem to have interrupted something special!' She wore a mischievous expression as she made this last remark.

Jonas smiled back at Nikki, who accompanied him to the door. 'Wait and see...' he repeated her own words concerning her own relationship.

'With bated breath,' his sister assured him. 'Mother can't wait to see her little baby married with children of his own!'

'Wait a minute!' He held up protesting hands. 'You're going way too fast for me. I've only just met—the woman,' he amended using Danie's name; it wasn't appropriate at the moment! 'Wives and babies do not figure too highly in my immediate plans!'

'Unless the first is in the singular, I wouldn't contemplate the latter at all!' Nikki pointed out. 'Bigamy is still a prosecutable offence, you know!'

'Don't get picky on me; you knew exactly what I meant!' Jonas bent and kissed his sister goodnight. 'I'll give you a call tomorrow,' he promised before strolling over to his car.

He thought briefly of lingering in the driveway to call Danie on his mobile, but, as his sister was still standing in the doorway waiting to wave goodbye, he thought better of it. Heaven knew what Nikki would make of his telephoning that certain someone as soon as he left her house!

Besides, he wasn't absolutely sure what to make of the impulse himself, he decided as he drove home. A carrying-out of his promise to Danie to call her later? Or a need to confirm, by just hearing the sound of Danie's no-nonsense voice, that she definitely wasn't the woman who had once been involved with Ben…?

Ridiculous, he told himself with a shake of his head; as if just hearing Danie speak could tell him that! He either believed it wasn't his Danie, or he didn't. It was as simple as that.

Although nothing seemed particularly simple when Jonas finally telephoned Danie's apartment fifteen minutes later—at almost midnight—to discover her line was already engaged!

Jonas's thought processes went into overdrive as he slowly replaced his own receiver. No one received casual telephone calls at this time of night. Which meant it was someone specific, someone Danie didn't mind talking to, no matter how late it was.

Ben…?

CHAPTER EIGHT

JONAS hadn't telephoned...!

That was the thought that occupied Danie's time most of the next day. Biking down to the estate. Flying her father and Audrey, recently returned from Scotland, to France. Waiting for him to conclude his business later in the day before flying them back again.

Of course, Jonas's omission could mean nothing.

Or it could mean everything...!

Damn it, why did these negative thoughts always intrude on her more positive ones?

Jonas had left last night to go and help his sister. It could have taken him a while to sort that situation out. Jonas might not have returned home until late and thought it inconsiderate to telephone her. He might have telephoned her today instead—and she had been out all day!

She had no reason—no reason at all!—to suppose she had come into the conversation last night between Jonas and his ex-brother-in-law.

Except Jonas hadn't telephoned, that taunting little voice reminded her for the hundredth time.

'Staying for dinner?' her father enquired once they had all arrived back at the house.

'Er—no,' Danie refused. 'I—er—I have to meet someone in town,' she answered evasively.

Her father raised an eyebrow. 'Anyone we know?'

Danie gave him a narrow-eyed look. 'Exactly what do you mean by that?'

'Actually...nothing,' her father returned slowly, frown-

113

ing thoughtfully as he poured a drink for Audrey and himself. 'But now that you mention it, why *did* you want Jonas's telephone—?'

'Leave the girl alone, Rome,' Audrey told him before accepting her glass of white wine. 'We're all entitled to our secrets.'

'Even you, Audrey?' Rome returned.

'Even me,' she replied enigmatically.

Rome looked less than pleased by this reply, Danie noted. As far as he was concerned, Danie knew, Audrey's job, and him, had to be her priorities in life—and not necessarily in that order!

'I have to go,' Danie told them. 'Helicopter to Yorkshire at ten o'clock tomorrow?' she confirmed.

Her father nodded distractedly, his gaze still resting thoughtfully on Audrey.

Well, at least the other woman had diverted his attention from her, Danie accepted gratefully. Although she wasn't sure Audrey had assured an easy evening for herself!

'I'll see you both in the morning, then,' Danie announced lightly, bending to kiss Audrey on the cheek before making a face at the older woman—a look that clearly said, 'Thanks. And good luck!'

Audrey gave an acknowledging smile before calmly taking a sip of her wine, her expression now as serene as always.

Danie held back a smile as she moved to kiss her father goodnight. She only hoped Audrey knew what she was doing; Rome could be relentless when he wanted to know something. And he was obviously interested in this private life Audrey had alluded to!

Danie's humour, however, evaporated as soon as she began the ride home. She hadn't been lying when she'd said she was meeting someone in town. But, unfortunately, it wasn't Jonas. And at the moment, he was the person she most wanted to see.

Maybe he would have left a message on her answer-machine? Although even if he hadn't, that didn't mean he hadn't called; some people, herself included, didn't actually like leaving messages on machines.

Stop making excuses, Danie, that little voice told her again. If Jonas wanted to telephone her, then no doubt he would do so. And she had no reason to believe, from the way they had parted last night, that he wouldn't want to.

She was absolutely shattered by the time she arrived back at her apartment, and the lack of flashes on her answer-machine told her there were no messages for her at all, adding to those feelings of exhaustion.

But she was expecting Andie here in half an hour, so she had no choice but to shower and change before her sister arrived. It would be nice to see her younger sister, although quite what the two of them were going to talk about, Danie had no idea; as far as she was aware, her younger sister still wasn't aware of their father's illness.

The best way to handle this, Danie decided as she blow-dried her hair after her shower, was to let Andie do the talking; after all, Andie was the one who had asked to come here, not the other way round.

Andie still looked far from well herself when Danie let her into her apartment twenty minutes later; her sister was still extremely pale, and she looked as if she had lost weight, too.

Although no less beautiful, Danie acknowledged affectionately. She was tall and blonde, with the same green-coloured eyes as her two older sisters, and Andie's illness and loss of weight had given her a certain air of fragility that Danie was sure a lot of men would find appealing.

'I know; I look like hell,' Andie said as she strolled into

the apartment, extremely elegant in a fitted black trouser suit and emerald-coloured silk blouse; it was a family joke that Andie had asked to wear designer-label clothes while still in her cradle!

'Actually, I was just thinking the opposite.' Danie closed the door before following her sister through to the sitting-room. 'Although maybe you really should think about seeing a doctor,' she added with concern, the brighter lighting of her sitting-room showing that Andie was bordering on gaunt rather than just delicate.

Her sister dropped down wearily into one of the armchairs. 'I've seen one,' she groaned.

'You have?' Danie didn't even attempt to hide her surprise. Andie had refused to see a doctor, unless absolutely necessary, since she'd been five years old and had had to go into hospital to have her tonsils out; she must really be feeling ill if she had actually taken herself to see one now!

'I have.' Andie nodded heavily. 'Would it be too much trouble to ask you for a cup of tea? Earl Grey, if you have it,' she asked hopefully. 'I've only just left the office, so I haven't even had time to go home yet.'

'Come through to the kitchen,' Danie gestured. 'Sit yourself down, while I make the tea,' she ordered as she heated the water on the Aga. 'Before you fall down,' she tacked on reprovingly as Andie looked even paler under the bright kitchen lights. 'You really shouldn't be working at all at the moment if you still feel this ill, Andie,' she scolded worriedly.

Her sister gave a wan smile. 'I've never understood how you got away with having that heavy thing up here.' She pointed in the direction of the Aga. 'It's amazing it hasn't gone through the floor into the flat downstairs before now!'

'Stop changing the subject, Andie.' Danie poured hot water into the warmed teapot. 'No wonder Rome is so worried about you,' she said; that worry certainly wasn't going to help his own ill health.

Andie's expression became guarded. 'What's Daddy been saying to you about me?'

'Nothing,' Danie answered truthfully, handing her sister the hot cup of tea. 'He doesn't need to say anything, I just know he's—concerned about you.'

Andie gave a sigh. 'That's one of his emotions, yes. But another one is—' She broke off as the security intercom rang from downstairs. 'Are you expecting anyone else?' Andie said with surprise.

No, she wasn't expecting anyone... But Danie couldn't deny that she was inwardly still hoping to hear from Jonas. Maybe he had decided to call round instead of telephoning?

'I'll just see who it is,' she responded, hurrying from the room before her sister could say anything further. Andie didn't look as if she were in the mood for visitors but, by the same token, Danie had no intention of sending Jonas away if her caller should turn out to be him.

If...

She pressed the button on the intercom. 'Yes?' she prompted guardedly.

'Danie, it's Jonas. Could I come—?'

'Yes!' Danie didn't wait to hear the rest of what he had to say, pressing the security button that would unlock the door downstairs, her hands shaking in her haste.

It *was* Jonas!

Her heart leapt at the thought of seeing him again. How she was going to deal with having him and Andie here at the same time, she had no idea, but no doubt she would find a way. She would have to!

She turned slowly as she heard her sister come through

from the kitchen. 'Feeling any better?' She delayed answering the question in her sister's expression.

'I don't expect to for some time,' Andie muttered, tilting her head enquiringly. 'Is that a blush I see on your cheeks, Danie?' she said slowly.

Flushed probably better described how she looked, Danie decided. At the thought of seeing Jonas again!

She moistened her lips. 'Andie, I—' The ringing of the doorbell stopped her from any further explanation. Jonas was here already! 'Just let me get that,' she told Andie breathlessly. 'And I'll explain everything later.'

Andie relented. 'Fine.'

Jonas looked wonderful to Danie as he stood on the threshold, dressed very casually in fitted denims and a dark blue cashmere sweater. Although his guarded expression didn't look too encouraging, she realised with a sinking heart.

'I hope I'm not interrupting anything,' he said politely.

Not as far as she was concerned, although she accepted Andie might not feel quite the same way!

'Of course not,' Danie assured him lightly, stepping back. 'Come in,' she invited warmly. After all, he could just look wary because he hadn't telephoned her last night and felt unsure of his welcome.

He *could* be, she told herself determinedly as doubts about that possibility instantly began to crowd into her head. Of course he could...

Although Danie certainly wasn't prepared for her sister's reaction to Jonas as he preceded Danie into the sitting-room!

'You!' Andie gasped as she stood up slowly, green eyes glaring. 'What are *you* doing here?' she demanded rudely.

Danie gaped. There was no other way to describe how

she just stood there with her mouth open at this unwarranted attack on Jonas. What on earth was her sister *doing*?

Andie turned accusingly to Danie. 'Did you invite him here?' she cried furiously, putting her cup and saucer down noisily onto the table. 'You had no right,' she continued shakily. 'Absolutely no right! Damn this family,' she muttered through gritted teeth. 'Damn you all!' Her hands were clenched tightly at her sides, her movements agitated.

Jonas drew in a controlling breath. 'Andrea—'

'Don't even try to find placating excuses for this—this intrusion!' Andie's head snapped back round to him as she butted in heatedly, the colour definitely back in her cheeks now. 'This is my problem, no one else's, and—'

'Your family is concerned for you,' Jonas soothed.

'Then they can damn well become unconcerned,' Andie snapped, bending to pick up her bag before marching towards the door. 'I never thought you would let me down in this way,' she paused to tell Danie, tears glistening in her eyes now. 'I accept Daddy has his reasons...' she continued brokenly. 'But not you, Danie.' She looked dazed. 'And as for sneaking around behind my back in this way—'

'But I—'

'Never mind,' Andie chokingly dismissed Danie's protest. 'Just another of life's little disappointments that I'll have to adjust to, I expect. I should have got used to them by now,' she added bitterly, shaking her head in disgust. 'I just never thought— Damn you, Danie,' she finished in a pained voice.

'Now just a minute.' Danie had had time to snap out of her own dumbstruck reaction to this unexpected turn of events—and now she wanted to know *what* was going on!

That Andie and Jonas already knew each other was

more than apparent, and Danie wanted to know exactly why and how that was!

'I have no idea what you're talking about, Andie,' she told her sister firmly. 'For one thing, I have no idea in what way you believe I have let you down.' It was something she would never do; the three sisters were completely loyal to each other, and their father. And as the youngest sister, Andie had always been more cosseted and protected by all of them.

Andie's mouth turned downwards. 'Maybe you don't see it as letting me down,' she replied. 'But why won't any of you understand that this has to be my decision, and my decision alone? And no amount of family pressure is going to change that! Now, if you don't mind, I think I had better leave. Before I insult—your guest, any further.' She gave a scathing glance in Jonas's direction. 'I don't believe, after tonight, that it's necessary for me to tell you I won't be attending my appointment with you tomorrow.'

Jonas looked less than pleased by this announcement, taking a step forward, his hand raised placatingly. 'Andrea—'

'I'll find myself another consultant, Mr Noble,' Andie told him with cold dismissal. 'One that I can trust,' she added bitterly.

Danie still had no real idea of what was happening here, although it had become obvious in the last few seconds that she had been completely wrong about her assumption that her father was Jonas's patient—obviously Andie was...!

She had never seen Andie like this; her younger sister had always been warmly charming, her looks impeccable. But Andie had been anything but polite to Jonas in the last few minutes, and, despite the fact that her sister was dressed as beautifully as ever, Andie did, in fact, look ex-

actly as she'd described herself on her arrival—'like hell'!
Whatever else was wrong with her, she was obviously very
ill…!

Danie turned accusing eyes on Jonas now. 'Are you just
going to let her walk out of here?' she demanded. 'Looking the way that she does?'

Jonas's hands dropped down ineffectually to his sides.
'I can only advise, Danie, I can't make Andrea do anything,' he reasoned flatly.

'Well, it's nice to know that at least one of you seems
to have realised that!' Andie broke in. 'I'll call you some
time, Danie,' she said. 'When I'm not quite so angry with
you. And I've made my mind up exactly what I want to
do.'

Danie watched as Andie let herself out of the apartment,
the door closing decisively behind her; Danie's mind was
buzzing with the things that had been said the last few
minutes.

Andie, not her father, was Jonas's patient.

But why?

What was wrong with her sister?

Oh, she knew Andie had had the flu several weeks ago,
and that her sister seemed to be having trouble bouncing
back to full health. But what, exactly, did that mean…?

Danie turned her questioning gaze on Jonas. 'Who are
you?' she breathed slowly. '*What* are you?' she added
hardly.

His cheeks were pale beneath his tan, the encounter of
the last few minutes obviously having taken its toll on him
too. But for the moment Danie was unconcerned with that.
Jonas knew the assumptions she had made concerning his
visit to the estate on Saturday—that she had believed her
father was the one who was ill—and he had let her go on
thinking that!

'Don't make me go to the trouble of finding out, Jonas,' she warned icily, starting to feel angry herself now.

Jonas had known from the beginning that she was seeing him in the hope that she could wheedle information out of him concerning what she had believed to be her father's illness. Hey, the two of them had even laughed together at her lack of success! And all the time Jonas had been laughing for an altogether different reason...

He drew in a ragged breath, his head back as he met her challenging expression. 'I don't suppose it matters now that Andrea has decided she no longer wishes to be my patient,' he said. 'I'm an obstetrician, Danie.'

An ob—

An obste—

Danie couldn't even bring herself to say the word. Because if that was what Jonas was, that meant that Andie—that Andie—

Oh, my goodness...!

Jonas watched Danie as he saw the truth finally sink into her rapidly racing brain—a truth she obviously found even more incredible than her former belief that her father was seriously ill.

He had known the assumption she had made on Saturday, of course he had. But, in the circumstances, with his professional loyalty based with his patient, what else could he have done but let her go on thinking that?

However, he could see now, as Danie's eyes began to glitter as angry a green as her younger sister's, a few minutes ago, that Danie wasn't in the least impressed by his professional etiquette!

'It wasn't my secret to tell, Danie,' he said wearily. 'It still isn't.'

'Oh, don't worry, Jonas,' Danie returned. 'You still

haven't told me anything! But I think, if you had just once mentioned your profession, I might have had an inkling my father wasn't involved in your medical examination on Saturday!' Her voice was thick with sarcasm.

This had all been rather a shock for her; Jonas realised that. But at the moment the anger Danie felt towards him was more to the forefront than the fact that her younger, unmarried sister was going to have a baby.

He couldn't exactly blame Danie for feeling that way, accepted that he had been less than helpful. At any other time he would have tried to placate her. It was just that engaged telephone line late the previous evening that held him back from attempting to get too close to her...

He hadn't slept well last night, his head full of thoughts of whom Danie could have been talking to on the telephone at that time of night. The idea that it could have been Ben, that Ben had decided to once again snap his fingers in Danie's direction, was an altogether unacceptable one to Jonas!

But the doubt that it just might have been his ex-brother-in-law had persisted, making today hell too as he'd tried to function normally and blot all thoughts of Danie from his head. Something he had only succeeded in doing for mere minutes at a time!

After picking at the dinner he had prepared for himself when he'd returned from the clinic, he had known that he had to at least see Danie. How he was going to ask her if she knew Ben, without it sounding like some sort of accusation, he had no idea, he had just known he had to speak to her face to face. As he knew only too well, Danie's emotions could be as transparent as glass on occasion.

This just wasn't going to be one of those occasions!

Oh, Danie was still transparent enough in her emotions,

and the one she was feeling most at the moment was anger—towards him! Not the ideal situation in which to ask her questions about her personal life before the two of them had met.

Jonas gave a humourless smile. 'Well, you know the truth of that visit now, so—'

'I still don't know anything that matters,' Danie cut in forcefully. 'Who? When? How?'

'I think we both know how, Danie,' Jonas gently answered her floundering questions. 'I don't know exactly when, although it's my belief the baby will be born some time around Valentine's day next year. As for the who...' he sighed '...I believe your father wants an answer to that particular question too.' He shrugged. 'But it isn't one Andrea feels like sharing with any of us.'

Danie shook her head, momentarily diverted from her anger towards him, her thoughts all inwards. 'Andie doesn't even have a regular boyfriend that I know of.' She seemed to be speaking to herself now. 'Let alone one that—' She broke off, glaring up at Jonas once again. 'Surely Andie must have told you *something*? Or would answering that come under the heading of breaching professional etiquette too?'

'It would. And it does,' Jonas replied evenly, inconsequentially noticing that the yellow roses he had brought her the evening before were arranged in a cut-glass vase on the coffee-table. After tonight the flowers would probably end up in the bin, he acknowledged ruefully. 'Danie, I think Andie is the one you should be talking to about this,' he continued. 'She—'

'She won't talk to me now,' Danie dismissed contemptuously. 'She thinks I'm in cahoots with you and my father!'

There was probably a lot of truth in that statement, but,

nevertheless, he still wasn't in a position to discuss Andrea Summer, not even with her concerned older sister.

Jonas raised his hands in defeat. 'Then I suggest you unconvince her,' he said mildly, realising as he did so that he was being less than helpful. But the truth of the matter was, he hadn't come here to talk about Andrea Summer...!

Danie continued to glare at him, tall and beautiful in a tight pale green tee shirt and bottle-green denims that moulded to her slender hips and thighs. A fact Jonas noted—and instantly berated himself for. He wasn't here to become enthralled in the way Danie looked.

Then what was he here for?

To ask a woman he had only known a matter of days, a woman he found himself very attracted to, a woman he liked—a woman he had come very close to making love to the previous evening!—if she had once had an affair with his sister's husband.

Great!

The realisation made even him wince—and he had been the one intent on asking such a question.

Well, it was a sure fact he couldn't ask it now—he would most likely end up with the vase of roses smashed over his head if he did!

'I'm sorry, Danie.' He sighed heavily. 'I know I'm not being very helpful,' he understated. 'But you obviously have a close relationship with Andrea; she wouldn't have been here otherwise— '

'No one ever calls her Andrea,' Danie told him distract-edly. 'And, after tonight, I think that closeness you're talking about may be a thing of the past,' she added bitterly. 'Andie called me, asked if she could come and have a chat—a chat I now believe probably involved her—preg-nancy.' She swallowed hard, obviously still having trouble coming to terms with the idea of her sister expecting a baby. 'And within minutes of her arrival here, before she even had a chance to say anything about what was bothering her—'

'I arrived and upset everything,' Jonas accepted.

Danie looked uncomfortable. 'I wasn't exactly going to say that—'

'Just think it, hmm?' he suggested.

'Maybe,' she conceded. 'Andie obviously has something on her mind.' She frowned. 'Is there a problem with the pregnancy? Is that it? Or aren't you allowed to tell me that, either?'

'If there was, I wouldn't be, no,' Jonas answered levelly. 'But as far as I can ascertain, Andr—Andie,' he amended dryly, 'is a normal, healthy, twenty-five-year-old woman— apart from a pretty ferocious bout of morning sickness, which will hopefully stop in a few weeks' time.'

'Then I don't understand,' Danie persisted. 'What—?'

Jonas carried on: 'Your sister is normal and healthy, Danie—but she is also unmarried, completely unattached, according to you; don't you think, in the circumstances, she might feel a few qualms about having this baby?' He couldn't make it any clearer than that without completely breaking a patient's, even an ex-patient's, confidence.

Danie looked at him searchingly, as the meaning of his words slowly became clear to her.

'Good Lord,' she breathed weakly, dropping down into one of the armchairs. 'Andie is thinking about not having this baby? Is that the decision she said is for her to make and her alone?'

'And wouldn't you say that it was?' Jonas said quietly, moving to pour Danie half an inch of whisky into one of the glasses that stood beside the drinks tray.

She took the glass gratefully, taking a reviving mouthful

of the fiery liquid. 'Of course it's for Andie to decide,' she finally spoke again. 'But—'

'In Andie's eyes there isn't a but, Danie,' Jonas told her kindly, coming down on his haunches beside the chair she sat in.

'Well...maybe not as far as the family is concerned,' she conceded. 'But the father—'

'Whoever he might be.'

Danie gave him a furious glare. 'I can assure you that if Andie is pregnant—'

'She most certainly is,' he confirmed, knowing this conversation had gone too far now for prevarication.

'Then Andie knows exactly who the father is,' Danie bit out.

'And she isn't telling,' Jonas pointed out, relieved to see Danie's anger had revived her.

Danie looked puzzled. 'Not even Rome?'

'Especially not Rome.'

'But why not? He'll have to know some time, we all will— If Andie decides to have the baby...' she realised faintly.

Jonas didn't know Andie very well, had met her only briefly on Saturday, when he had carried out his examination to confirm her pregnancy. But if Andie was anything like her older sister, and he had reason to believe she was, then she would make her own mind up about the future—without any interference from anyone!

'I have to go to her,' Danie decided suddenly, putting down the whisky glass before standing up. 'I'm sorry, Jonas.' She turned back in time to see him regaining his balance after almost being knocked off his feet by her sudden ascent. 'Doubly sorry,' she apologised as she realised what she had done. 'But I have to go out. I'm sure you understand?' She moved swiftly about the apartment picking up her jacket, handbag and car keys.

Oh, he understood. All too well. Danie was responding exactly as he had last night when his sister had needed him, exactly as Danie had said she would if the positions were reversed. But there was still so much unresolved between the two of them. Whether or not Danie knew Ben, for one thing... For the main thing!

Danie hesitated in the action of pulling on her jacket. 'I forgot to ask—did everything go okay with your own sister last night?' she asked guardedly—almost as if she had picked up on at least some of his thoughts.

Or was he just looking for some sort of guilty reaction in her? Quite honestly, he didn't know any more. 'Fine,' he responded, not willing to go any deeper into last night until he was more sure of Danie. 'I did call you,' he confessed, again watching her closely.

'You did?' Danie echoed. 'But I have a telephone next to my bed, and—'

'The number was engaged,' Jonas replied.

Again he watched for Danie's reaction, and for a few moments she just continued to look puzzled, and then her brow—that smooth alabaster brow—cleared. 'It was Andie,' she said heavily. 'I should have known when she telephoned me so late at night that there was something seriously wrong,' she admonished herself.

Andie...? It had been her *sister* on the telephone at almost midnight last night?

Or was she just saying that—?

God. Jonas reeled at the sickening realisation that his suspicions concerning Danie and Ben had gone so deep. Too deep to be ignored or forgotten, even though it had been her sister talking to her on the telephone last night...?

The truth of the matter was, he couldn't bear the thought

of any other man being involved with Danie, let alone a man he had nothing but contempt for!

Which meant precisely what?

'I really do have to go, Jonas,' Danie cut sharply into his muddled thoughts. 'It may take me some time to even persuade Andie into letting me into her apartment, let alone actually talking to me about any of this.'

'Yes. Fine,' he responded abruptly, pushing away those disturbing thoughts about why he felt so jealously possessive of even Danie's past. 'I— We can talk again some other time.'

'Yes.' Danie looked across at him guardedly. 'Well. We had better go, then,' she prompted awkwardly.

Part of him wanted to go. But another part of him just wanted to forget all the complications that seemed to be pushing them apart, to just sweep Danie into his arms and make love to her, forget all about—

But he couldn't forget. Even though he now knew it had been Andie on the telephone late last night, his suspicions concerning Ben and the 'Danie' he had mentioned persisted.

'Yes,' he agreed flatly.

Neither of them spoke as they travelled downstairs in the lift together, standing feet apart, a wall seeming to have dropped down between the two of them. And it was getting higher with each passing minute.

'Can I drop you anywhere?' he offered once they were outside on the pavement, his car parked across the road.

'No, thank you,' Danie refused, not quite meeting his eyes as she looked somewhere over his left shoulder. 'I may be some time,' she continued, 'and I'll need transport home.'

'Of course,' Jonas replied. 'I—I hope your meeting with Andie goes well.'

She smiled humourlessly. 'So do I.' Her tone implied she didn't hold out much hope of that, but that she had to try nonetheless.

'Goodnight, then,' he said—having the terrible feeling that it *was* actually goodbye!

Danie's eyes glistened brightly green as she looked up at him at last.

Almost as if she had tears in her eyes, Jonas realised. But that was ridiculous. Why on earth should Danie be on the verge of tears?

'Goodnight, Jonas,' she said quickly before turning on her heel and walking away, disappearing around the corner of the building seconds later on her way to the private car park at the back.

It *had* been goodbye. For both of them, Jonas thought sadly. Danie couldn't forgive him for not telling her that her father wasn't his patient. And he—he couldn't get by the fact that Danie might have had an affair with his brother-in-law!

The aching pain in his heart at that realisation told him exactly why he was so jealous of Danie's past as well as her future—he was in love with her!

CHAPTER NINE

'YOU'RE extremely quiet this morning,' Danie's father commented interestedly.

Danie didn't even turn from her attention on the controls of the helicopter as they flew above the English countryside, her father seated beside her, Audrey in the back. 'I thought you didn't like chattering women in the morning,' she replied dryly.

'A hello might have been nice,' her father said disgruntledly.

'Hello,' Danie said with dry sarcasm.

The truth of the matter was, she was not in the mood for polite pleasantries. Last night had not been very successful—on any front!—and she blamed her father for at least some of that. She was twenty-seven years old, for goodness' sake, surely old enough for him to have confided in her about Andie.

As it was, she had arrived at her sister's apartment late last night to find that Andie had already been there and gone again, leaving with a small overnight bag, according to the building's security guard.

A few telephone calls to some of Andie's friends when she'd returned to her own home had told Danie that her sister wasn't with any of them, and she couldn't be with Harrie and Quinn, either, because they were still away. So at this precise moment, she had no idea where her sister was—and so she was not in the mood to be polite to their father!

'I know about Andie, Rome,' she told him coolly.

'Oh.'

'"Oh"?' she repeated sharply. 'Is that all you can say?' She turned blazing green eyes on him. 'My little sister is in the biggest mess of her life, and all you can say is "oh"?' she accused, two bright spots of colour in her cheeks now.

'No, that isn't all I can say,' her father bit back angrily. 'But as Andie has told me all too frequently this last week, she's a big girl now, and I—'

'She's disappeared,' Danie cut in cruelly, knowing that she wasn't being completely fair. Like Jonas, her father had been entrusted with a confidence, and it wasn't for him to break it.

Jonas...!

He knew about her and Ben. Danie didn't know *how* he knew, she only knew that he did. She had seen it in his eyes last night, had felt it in the distance he kept between them. And, angry as she was with the fact that Jonas had let her carry on believing it was her father who was seriously ill, it was a distance that she didn't feel like closing at the moment, either.

After all, what did it matter? she had told herself determinedly as she had gone to bed last night. She hardly knew Jonas, their acquaintance was of only a few days' standing; she would get over the feelings she had for him. She would have to!

'What do you mean, Andie's disappeared?' her father demanded tautly. 'How—?'

'She came to my apartment last night, there was a scene, she left,' Danie told him economically.

Rome frowned. 'What sort of scene? What did you do or say to upset her—?'

'I didn't do or say anything,' Danie came back furiously. 'She—'

'Might I suggest the two of you just calm down?' Audrey spoke soothingly from behind them. 'You both love Andie; I'm sure neither of you would ever do anything to hurt her.'

'Thank you for your vote of confidence, Audrey,' Danie accepted tensely before turning back to her father. 'Andie left last night because—' she broke off momentarily '—Jonas called round, and Andie jumped to the conclusion I was in league with the both of you, and—'

'Jonas called round...?' Rome repeated. 'Just how long has Jonas Noble been in the habit of calling round to your apartment?'

'Since I invited him to do so,' she snapped. 'But that isn't important—'

'I beg to differ,' her father interrupted. 'I think it's very important.'

'Why?' she challenged, her hands tight on the controls.

'Why? I'm sure he must be breaching some sort of medical etiquette—'

'Jonas hasn't breached anything,' Danie assured him—before he dared to ask her a personal question that she certainly wasn't going to answer! 'Besides, Andie is no longer his patient,' she added reluctantly.

'You know something, Danie,' her father spoke mildly—too mildly!—resting his head back against the leather seat, although he was far from relaxed, 'I think you might have been right about my feelings concerning chattering women in the mornings! This last five minutes of conversation has given me a headache!'

She had known her father wasn't going to like Andie's decision to dismiss Jonas as her consultant. She had also known he wasn't going to like the fact that Andie had taken herself off without telling anyone.

The fact that he was also not exactly pleased that she

had been seeing Jonas was totally irrelevant; after last night, she doubted she would be seeing Jonas ever again!

And if, at the moment, that caused her some pain, it was a pain she was going to keep to herself. Jonas could have told her something, anything, damn him, to alleviate the worry he knew she had felt over her father. As far as she was concerned, he had simply chosen not to do so, and it was a choice—the past and Ben apart—that ended any sort of relationship between them.

Just another relationship that hadn't worked out, that was how she would think of it one day. One day...

'Danie, turn this helicopter around and fly us back to the estate,' her father ordered suddenly, sitting up in his seat as he once again took charge. 'Audrey, telephone and cancel our appointment for this morning. Family commitments,' he instructed. 'We have to find Andie,' he explained as Danie looked at him with a puzzled expression.

'And if she doesn't wish to be found?' Danie had already turned the helicopter around as per her father's instruction.

'I'll find her anyway,' Rome assured her determinedly. 'That's my grandchild she's carrying!'

And Danie's niece or nephew... 'Andie will make the right choice in the end, you'll see,' she said with certainty.

'Just fly, Danie,' her father ground out harshly, obviously more shaken about Andie's disappearance than he cared to admit.

She flew, and she didn't linger at the estate once they had returned, either. If her father wanted to hunt Andie down, then he was welcome to do so. Danie felt she knew Andie well enough to know that her sister wouldn't do anything stupid or impulsive; Andie just needed time and space from family pressure to get her thoughts in order. At least, Danie hoped that was all it was!

The light was flashing on her answer-machine when she got in. Two messages. Maybe one of them would be from Andie!

'Danie, it's Jonas—Jonas Noble,' the first message played. 'Could you contact me on the following number as soon as possible?' He repeated the telephone number twice after the initial message before ringing off.

The fact that he had called didn't cheer Danie at all, in fact she just felt angry all over again. There had been no reason for him to say it was Jonas Noble; just how many Jonases did he think she knew? Dozens, probably, if he believed, as she thought he did, that she had once been involved with a married man.

She played the second message. 'Miss Summer, this is Mr Noble's secretary,' the brisk female voice informed her. 'It's very important that you contact him as soon as possible.' The message ended there.

If the first message had angered her, then the second one worried her. Jonas's call couldn't have been a personal one if he had got his secretary to call again some time later. There was only one reason she could think of for Jonas telephoning her on a business level.

Andie...?

She frantically rewound the tape, playing back the initial message, noting down the telephone number this time; she hadn't bothered the first time around, because she had thought Jonas had been calling on his own behalf. At the moment, they had nothing to say to each other on a personal level!

'Dorothy Quentin, Mr Noble's secretary,' came the reply to Danie's hurriedly made call. 'How may I help you?'

Danie didn't need to be told who the other woman was, easily recognised that brisk tone. 'It's Danie Summer,' she returned politely. 'You rang me earlier.'

'Ah, yes, Miss Summer.' The woman's tone softened slightly. 'Just hold the line a moment.'

'But—' Too late, the other woman had already put her on hold.

'Danie?' The rich tones of Jonas's voice came down the line seconds later.

'Yes,' she returned tersely. She had hoped to speak to his secretary, find out what the problem was, and go on from there. Actually speaking to Jonas had not been in her immediate plans.

'I have Andie here at my clinic—'

'Is she all right?' Danie's hand tightly gripped the receiver in her panic, waves of worried sickness washing over her.

'She is now,' he came back smoothly. 'She asked me to call you. She wants to see you.'

Danie barely had time to register the fact that Jonas obviously wouldn't have called her if Andie hadn't asked him to do so... She didn't have the time to think of that now. Explanations could come later, when she had ascertained for herself that Andie really was okay.

'I'll come straight away,' she told him without hesitation. 'My father—'

'Andie doesn't want him told just yet,' Jonas put in firmly. 'And, in the circumstances, I think that might be for the best.'

What circumstances? Danie wanted to demand. But didn't. Because, she knew from experience, Jonas wouldn't tell her anything!

Her mouth tightened. 'Give me the address, and I'll be there as quickly as possible.'

Jonas gave her the address of the private clinic. 'But don't break any speed limits—or your neck!—to get here,' he cautioned dryly.

As if he cared, Danie fumed inwardly. 'I wouldn't give you the satisfaction!' she told him forthrightly, ringing off before he could make a reply.

If he would have made one. Which Danie doubted. Whatever had been between Jonas and herself, it was over. And had been so since last night.

She didn't break any speed limits, or her neck, on the drive to the clinic, having decided to go on her bike instead of her car, which enabled her to weave in and out of the traffic. Although she felt a little conspicuous dressed in her black leathers, her crash-helmet tucked under her arm, as she strolled into the plush reception of the clinic!

'Private', in this case, was represented by rich and sumptuous, thick blue carpet on the floor, chairs of pale cream, paintings which adorned the cream walls, and a pretty receptionist who was seated behind a wide mahogany desk.

If the young woman was surprised at Danie's appearance, then she didn't show it, but smiled up at her enquiringly. 'Can I help you?' she offered brightly.

Danie opened her mouth to reply, but before she could do so an older woman came bustling through the double doors that had to lead through to the clinic. Her red hair showed signs of grey, although her blue eyes were lively enough as she came straight over to Danie.

'Miss Summer?' the woman greeted with a smile. 'I'm Dorothy Quentin, Jonas's secretary.'

Again Danie didn't need to be told that; she had recognised the voice. What she was surprised about was the fact that this woman had obviously been waiting for her arrival...

'I saw you arrive on the security camera,' Dorothy Quentin explained at Danie's frown, indicating the camera above the reception desk. 'Unfortunately, a very necessary fixture in this day and age. Would you like to come straight through and see your sister?' Not by the flicker of an eyelid did the woman show that Danie's appearance in biking leathers was unusual amongst visitors to the clinic.

Plus, Danie was here for no other reason than to see her sister…!

'Jonas will come through and talk to you in a few minutes when you've had time to say hello to your sister,' Dorothy Quentin told her as the two of them walked down the long carpeted corridor, closed doors leading off either side. 'He asked me to apologise for being delayed, but he shouldn't be too long.'

Danie didn't care where he was, or if he came and talked to her at all; she only wanted to see Andie and reassure herself her sister was okay.

'Could I have some coffee or tea brought through to you?' the older woman offered as she came to a halt outside one of the doors.

'Coffee would be nice.' Danie spoke for the first time since Dorothy Quentin had walked in and taken charge of the situation.

'Fine.' Dorothy smiled. 'Your sister is in this room here.' She indicated the closed door behind her before bustling off in search of the requested coffee.

Danie hesitated outside the door, having no idea what she was going to find once she went inside. Andie had told Jonas the previous evening that he was no longer her consultant, and yet she was here at his clinic now. To Danie's mind, that boded ill.

She drew in a deep breath, knocking lightly on the door before going inside.

'They aren't very alike, are they?' Dorothy opined as she strolled unannounced into Jonas's consulting-room.

Jonas sat behind his desk, looking up from the papers he had been trying to concentrate on. Trying—because he hadn't been succeeding; Danie was still very much in his thoughts. Even more so since he had admitted her sister to the clinic.

'Who aren't?' He frowned at his secretary's enigmatic comment.

'The two Summer sisters,' Dorothy said impatiently. 'Danie just arrived,' she announced.

Jonas sat up straighter in his high-backed leather chair. 'She did?' He tried to sound only mildly interested—but he knew from the knowing glitter in Dorothy's eyes that he had failed.

Dorothy nodded. 'And very fetching she looked too. If I thought it would do the same thing for my figure I might take to wearing leather,' she added speculatively.

It took tremendous effort to keep his expression deadpan as an all-too-disturbing vision of Danie in those leathers came into his head, every shapely curve shown to perfection. 'It wouldn't,' he assured Dorothy dryly.

Dorothy appeared unperturbed by his bluntness. 'She has gorgeous hair too,' she said enviously. 'In fact, she's absolutely beautiful,' she finished approvingly.

Danie was many things, beautiful being only one of them. Until two days ago he had believed Danie to be one of those rare people, who was beautiful inside as well as out; he had thought she had the same idea of family values as he did himself. But an affair with a married man told a completely different story...!

Because he simply couldn't get away from that fact, no matter how hard he had tried to believe it couldn't have been this particular Danie. Because he had seen the apprehension in her eyes the previous evening, as if she'd been waiting for a blow. Or an accusation...! That same wariness he had seen in her face the night he'd mentioned there were complications to their having a relationship. He was very much afraid now that wariness had been because for a moment, a very brief moment, Danie had thought he'd meant Ben...!

Jonas stood up. 'Is she with her sister now?'

'She is.' Dorothy answered slowly, noting his abrupt tone. 'I had coffee sent in for both of them.'

Dorothy's expression spoke of unasked questions Jonas was not going to answer!

He nodded. 'I'll go through and see them now. You may as well go to lunch now, Dorothy,' he advised her, not wanting to give her any excuse to have to come into Andrea Summer's room while he was talking to Andie and Danie.

She regarded him speculatively. 'Will you still be here when I get back or will you be taking an early lunch yourself?'

He tensed at her attempt to find out if he intended going out to lunch with Danie once they had both visited her sister, and before his next appointment. He didn't have any intention of lunching with Danie, of course, but sometimes Dorothy kept altogether too maternal an eye on his private life.

'I have no idea whether I will still be here when you return from lunch,' he answered impatiently. 'But I'm sure you have plenty of work to keep you busy if I've already left.'

Dorothy's brows rose at his biting tone. 'Your bedside manner could use a little polishing today,' she told him waspishly.

He sighed. 'I'm not at a bedside yet.'

'Probably as well,' came his secretary's parting comment.

Jonas's second sigh was even heavier than the first. After the way the two of them had said goodbye the evening before, he hadn't expected to see Danie again quite so soon. Although he accepted it was slightly different today; this was his territory, and Danie had only been invited on to it.

Nevertheless, he wasn't looking forward to seeing her again, and took a deep breath before walking briskly into Andrea Summer's room.

The two sisters turned at his entrance. Andie was lying in bed, Danie was sitting in a chair at her side. Dorothy was right: the two sisters were unalike to look at—except for those beautiful green eyes. Right now, their expressions were totally different: Andie was warmly welcoming; Danie glared at him with hostile dislike.

'Danie.' He nodded a terse greeting before turning to smile gently at Andie. 'How are you feeling now?'

'Much better,' she answered with certainty. 'My little scare has answered a lot of questions that have been worrying me. Most of all, it's made me realise I want to have this baby very much,' she admitted emotionally.

Andie's little scare had been the commencement of pains during the night as she'd lain in bed at the hotel she had booked into so that she could avoid her family. Jonas had been the only person she'd been able to think of calling at the time to help her. Which he had been only too happy to do.

Luckily those pains hadn't been as serious as Andie had feared, although Jonas still wanted her to stay at the clinic for a few days for observation.

'That's wonderful!' Danie told her sister huskily. Squeezing Andie's hand reassuringly. 'And when you want us, the family will all be there for you.'

This woman presented a dichotomy, Jonas inwardly reflected. She was one hundred per cent loyal to her family, and yet, at the same time, she had been instrumental in breaking up another family because of her relationship with another woman's husband. No matter how he tried, Jonas couldn't get past that fact...

And he had tried; oh, how he had tried! But Nikki's months of unhappiness after she and Ben had parted were something he could never forget.

Or that look of triumphant certainty on Ben's face when he'd left Nikki's home the other evening...!

He turned back to Danie with glacial eyes. 'I'm glad you were finally able to come and be with your sister,' he bit out harshly.

Those green eyes narrowed at his barely concealed sarcasm. 'Unfortunately I was at work when you telephoned,' Danie answered just as coldly. 'I came as soon as I received your message.'

Jonas looked her up and down. 'Unconventional as ever, I see,' he referred disparagingly to the tightly fitting biking leathers she wore.

But she looked absolutely stunning with her long red hair flowing down the length of her spine, the leather suit fitting her like a glove. So much so that Jonas was sure she couldn't possibly be wearing anything underneath. Which conjured up all sorts of erotic pictures in his head. Damn it!

Danie gave an acknowledging inclination of her head, obviously holding on to her own fiery temper with effort. Jonas could easily guess the reason for that too; it had nothing to do with not insulting him in return, and everything to do with not upsetting her sister.

'Strange,' Danie said evenly, obviously unable to completely refrain from making some sort of comment, 'but I feel some of that impatience with humanity coming over me once again!' She looked across at him challengingly.

Jonas met her challenging gaze unblinkingly. 'Perhaps you need feeding once again,' he drawled unconcernedly.

Her mouth thinned scathingly. 'I can wait,' she snapped, eyes flashing brilliantly green.

'Please don't do so on my account.' Andie stretched luxuriously in the comfort of the bed. 'I think I would like to have a little sleep.' She gave a smile. 'All this excitement has made me tired. So if the two of you want to go off and have some lunch together...' she added expectantly.

The verbal fencing he and Danie had been engaged in was not conducive to them wanting to go off and have a meal together; they would both end up with indigestion!

'Unfortunately, I have to be somewhere else in just over an hour.' Jonas spoke to Andie rather than Danie.

'Don't let us keep you.' Danie was the one to answer him with hard dismissal.

His eyes narrowed at her deliberately condescending tone. 'Perhaps I could have a few words with you before I leave...?' he suggested silkily.

'Go ahead,' she invited.

'Not here, if you don't mind,' he returned smoothly, turning to open the door. 'I'm sure Andie will benefit from being left alone for a while so that she can take that nap.'

'Please go ahead,' Andie told Danie dreamily, already half-asleep.

Leaving Danie no choice but to precede Jonas out of the room! But she did it with obvious reluctance, every inch of her body tense with resentment.

She turned angrily to face him once they were outside in the carpeted corridor. 'I hope what you're going to say has something to do with Andie's condition.'

By not so much of the flicker of an eyelid did he show how affected he was by how magnificent Danie looked when she was angry. It might be a hackneyed line, but in Danie's case it was certainly true; her hair seemed to spark with flame, her eyes flashed deeply green, and as for her body—! Her breasts were pert beneath the black leather, legs long and shapely as she adopted a determined stance.

'What else could it be?' he prompted softly.

Two bright spots of colour appeared in her alabaster cheeks. 'Is Andie going to be all right now?'

'As long as she takes things easy,' he replied. 'The fact that she seems to have come to a decision about the rightness of the pregnancy will take some of the strain off her. Of course, it would probably be better for her if she had a partner to share this with, but—'

'Having a man in your life usually brings more problems, not less!' Danie pronounced scornfully.

'In your experience?' Jonas pointed out.

She drew in a sharp breath before replying. 'In my experience, yes,' she finally answered with suppressed rage. 'Why don't you just say what you want to say, Jonas, and get this over with?' She looked at him with blazing eyes, her body tense, her hands clenched about the crash-helmet she held in front of her.

Almost as if it were a protective shield...? Which was ridiculous; Danie was more than capable of taking care of herself, in any sort of confrontation.

He had stiffened at the directness of her challenge. What did he want to say? If he were to ask her if she had once been involved with Ben, and she said yes—!

He shrugged. 'I have no idea what you're talking about, Danie.' He gave a pointed glance at his wrist-watch. 'And I really do have to go now.'

She looked exasperated. 'Another wealthy patient you have to go and pander to?'

Jonas straightened at her deliberately insulting tone, wondering what Danie would have to say if she knew he was going to a rather dilapidated clinic in a run-down part of the city, that he went there two afternoons of the week, and that, far from being pandered to, his patients there were much more in need of advice on how to subsist well enough to bring a healthy child into the world than anything else. But he only wondered what she would think—because he had no intention of telling her anything about where he was going! The relationship was no longer close enough for him to want to confide anything in her.

'Something like that,' he finally replied. 'In the circumstances, your sister will be staying in for a few days' observation, so perhaps I'll see you here again,' he added politely.

'Perhaps you will,' Danie answered shortly.

Jonas hesitated, knowing that if he walked away now, left things as they were, then it was all over between Danie and himself. But, then, wasn't it all over now anyway? The two of them were more like opponents eyeing each other across the ring than the lovers they had almost become.

'Take care, then, Danie.'

'I always do,' she returned stiltedly.

But still Jonas didn't make any physical move to leave. What was wrong with him? His mind was telling him to turn and walk away, but another part of him—a part he didn't seem to have control over at the moment!—didn't want to go.

Could Danie really have been involved in an affair with Ben? What if he were wrong about that? What if—?

'Goodbye, Jonas,' Danie cut in on his thoughts, finality in her tone.

He wasn't wrong, and they both knew it...

'Goodbye, Danie,' he echoed softly, turning and walking away this time.

And he didn't look back.

Even though every part of him wanted to do just that!

CHAPTER TEN

'WE'RE all very relieved that you're going to be all right now, Andie,' Rome said warmly.

'But...?' Andie added, eyeing him ruefully from the bed where she lay resting.

Danie had caught that 'but' in their father's tone too. As she sat beside her sister's bed, she couldn't say she was any more happy about it than Andie appeared to be. The most important thing was that Andie, after a day spent resting, now looked better than she had for weeks, and the main reason for that was the realisation that she really wanted this baby. To Danie, her sister's happiness and welfare were all that mattered.

But knowing how worried Rome had been this morning, Danie realised he had to be informed of Andie's whereabouts some time, and at her sister's request she had telephoned him with the news. Only to have him arrive at the clinic within an hour of her call!

Rome stood in front of the window now, the brightness of the evening sun shining behind him making it hard to discern his expression. 'It might help if we knew who the father is,' he rasped.

'Why?' Danie was the one to defensively answer him.

'Surely it's obvious?' Rome replied.

'Not to me,' Danie told him decisively.

'Danie believes men can be an unnecessary complication,' Jonas put in from the back of the room. 'To any situation!'

She turned to give him a narrow-eyed glare. She had no

147

idea what he was doing in here in the first place. Admittedly, this was his clinic, and Andie had obviously decided he should be her consultant after all—but Danie had no idea why he should be present during this meeting between Andie and their father; she was only here herself at Andie's request.

'I'm well aware of my daughter Danie's opinion of men, thank you, Jonas,' Rome retorted. 'Although it should be an opinion she had long grown out of,' he continued, for Danie's benefit alone. 'But, in this case, I'm afraid I have to agree with that opinion; without a man being involved, there would be no—complication!'

'What a way to describe your future grandchild, Daddy,' Andie chided mockingly.

'I can see you're feeling much better!' her father commented.

'Much,' Andie agreed with a self-satisfied smile.

Danie had spent most of the day with her younger sister, and they had talked most things through—the father of the baby being the exception. But, unlike their own father, Danie wasn't particularly interested in his identity. He didn't appear to have been of any help to Andie so far, so why involve him now?

But at least Andie believed her now about not being in cahoots with their father and Jonas. Although her sister had been speculative about exactly what Jonas had been doing at Danie's apartment yesterday evening... It was speculation Danie did not intend satisfying!

Jonas had been in to check on Andie several times during the late afternoon and early evening, and for the main part Danie had ignored him. The fact that he ignored her too had rankled rather than upset her.

'I'm sure it would be beneficial to Jonas if he were to

know who the baby's father is,' Rome persisted. 'Wouldn't it?' he asked Jonas pointedly.

'It might be of some help,' Jonas replied guardedly.

'In what way?' Danie flew into the exchange.

Jonas turned his hard brown gaze on her. 'From a health point of view, of course,' he returned smoothly.

He knew of her resentment at his presence, and was responding to it. Good! Danie wanted him to know exactly how much she now resented him. He could think what he liked. After the way Jonas had let her carry on believing it was her father who was the one who was ill, she certainly wasn't in a mood to defend her actions of two years ago. She could come to regret that decision later on, but at the moment she was just too fed up to care!

'You've already told us that Andie is perfectly healthy, that the twinges she felt during the night weren't serious,' Danie persisted.

'I was referring to the baby's health, of course,' Jonas patiently responded. 'The age and health of the father can often be a good indication of other things.'

Danie gave a disbelieving snort. 'I hope you're not implying that my sister may have been involved with a sickly geriatric!' she exclaimed, with an amused look at the beautiful Andie.

Andie gave a throaty chuckle. 'Thanks for that vote of confidence, Danie!' She grinned. 'Is that what's been worrying you too, Rome? That the baby's father may be someone totally unsuitable?'

'I'm glad you now find all of this so funny!' Rome muttered impatiently.

'Not exactly, Daddy.' Andie sobered. 'It's just such a relief to know that everything is going to be okay.'

'Of course it is.' Danie gave her hand a reassuring squeeze before sparing the time to give the two men a reproachful glare. 'And I'm sure Andie would like to have another rest—now that you've satisfied yourself as to her welfare.'

Rome drew in a harsh breath, obviously having difficulty holding back his usual drive to take control of a situation. Because this was a situation of which Andie had made it more than plain she wouldn't let him be in control!

'Don't you agree, Jonas?' Danie went on. After all, he was supposed to be the specialist around here.

'I think that's up to Andie,' he replied noncommittally. 'As I've learnt only too well, the Summer women are a law unto themselves—and God help anyone who gets in their way!'

Danie gave him a sharp look, knowing that she had to be the one responsible for forming most of his opinion of the Summer women.

Was that really what he thought—or was he just referring to what he believed to be the truth of her past involvement with Ben? Did he believe that she hadn't cared that his sister was in the way of that relationship, that she had conducted an affair with Ben in spite of his wife and two young children? Jonas didn't know her very well at all if that was the conclusion he had come to...

'You're right there, Jonas,' Rome agreed with him wearily. 'I sometimes sit and wonder where I went wrong...'

'Or right,' Danie put in, standing up, no longer wearing her leathers, having returned briefly to her apartment during the afternoon to change into some lighter clothes; her red tee shirt and black denims were much more suitable for the heating necessary in the clinic. 'Time we were all going, I think,' she declared. Andie, for one, looked as if she had had enough for one evening!

Danie wasn't far behind her. It had been a long and difficult day, not helped by Jonas popping in and out when he'd come in to check on Andie, and Danie longed to get back to the peace and quiet of her apartment. To lick her own wounds in private...

She bent and kissed Andie warmly on the cheek. 'Don't worry,' she whispered for her sister's ears alone. 'I'll keep Daddy off your back,' she promised.

'And how do you intend doing that?' Andie whispered back. Both of them knew their father too well to believe he would ever stay in the background of any situation that involved his daughters.

Danie grinned. 'I'll think of something!'

'I wish you luck.' Andie squeezed her hand gratefully.

'What are you two girls whispering about together there?' their father demanded impatiently behind them. 'The three of them used to gang up on me when they were younger,' he informed Jonas wryly. 'I never stood a chance!'

'I can believe that,' Jonas acknowledged dryly.

Danie straightened, shooting him a look that said she didn't care what he believed—about anything!

'Could I have a word with you?' Jonas asked once the three of them were in the corridor outside Andie's room.

It took Danie several seconds to realise he was actually talking to her, looking up to find his steady gaze on her. She frowned resentfully. 'Which word would that be?' she challenged—sure he had a whole selection he could choose from for what he believed her to be!

'I think it's time I was on my way,' Rome announced after a glance at their two set faces. 'I'll need you at the estate at nine o'clock tomorrow morning,' he told Danie.

She didn't turn to look at her father, locked in a battle of wills with Jonas, both of them refusing to break the glance, hard brown eyes clashing with gold green. 'I'll be there,' she answered her father evenly.

'Fine. Thanks for everything, Jonas,' Rome said. 'I— Oh, to hell with it,' he muttered as neither of the adversaries spared even so much as a glance his way, stomping off down the corridor on his way out.

Adversaries... Was that what she and Jonas now were? It would appear so, her own will implacable, Jonas tight-mouthed and hard-eyed.

'I believe we may have upset your father.' Jonas finally spoke.

Danie shrugged. 'He'll get over it,' she dismissed. 'A word, I believe you said...?'

'In my office,' Jonas stated, looking as if he were about to take hold of her arm, and then thought better of it, his own hand falling ineffectually back to his side. 'If you would like to come this way,' he told her tightly before striding off down the corridor.

She didn't like it at all, but there was always the possibility that this word he wanted to have with her could be about Andie. Danie doubted it, of course, but she would listen to what he had to say anyway. And then she would react.

There was no doubting that Jonas looked more distant and unapproachable in the formal suit he wore today than she had ever seen him before, the deference with which he was treated by the staff here an indication of the respect he commanded. But, as far as Danie was concerned, that air of distance that surrounded Jonas could only be a bonus. She did not want to think of him as the man she had almost made love with two nights ago!

No doubt he was excellent at his job and therefore deserving of the deference shown him by his staff, Danie acknowledged; it was only as a human being that he was found wanting!

His office, obviously also his consulting-room, was as

plush as the rest of the clinic, but Danie spared it hardly a glance as she refused the seat he offered her opposite his across the desk. She wasn't a subordinate about to be chastised by her superior!

'Could you make this quick? I have to be somewhere else.' She sarcastically repeated the excuse he had made to her this morning before leaving.

Was it her imagination, or had he stiffened at this statement?

Damn it, he had. Did he think she was still involved with Ben—was that it? Or did he think there was some other man she was meeting, despite her telling him there wasn't anyone in her life?

Damn him!

She hadn't so much as looked at a man the last two years, had been so hurt and humiliated at the discovery of Ben's deceit that she had become sceptical and wary of all men after that, never wanting to find herself in such an unacceptable—to her!—position, ever again.

She had been surprised herself, after the shaky start to their own relationship, to find herself attracted to Jonas, to such an extent that she had allowed him to slip beneath the wall of reserve she had built about her emotions. And look where it had got her!

'I won't keep you long,' Jonas grated. 'But you made a comment to me earlier today for which I would like an explanation.' He looked at her with narrowed eyes.

'Yes?' she prompted, wondering which one of her cutting comments that could have been!

'Something about not giving me the satisfaction of breaking your neck on the drive over here this morning.'

That had been during their telephone conversation this morning, for goodness' sake. And Jonas had waited all day to ask her what she meant by it...? Somehow she found that hard to believe. Which begged the question: why had he really delayed her departure a few minutes ago...?

'I was referring, of course, to the fact that you wish you had never met me—'

'I don't believe I have ever said—'

'And that equally,' she continued, 'I wish I had never met you! Oh, you didn't exactly lie to me, Jonas, except by omission, but nonetheless you did let me carry on believing something you knew to be untrue. Namely, that my father was ill.'

'You—'

'Whereas you—' again she continued as if Jonas hadn't tried to interrupt '—on even less evidence than I had, believe I've done a similar thing where you're concerned!' Her head went back challengingly, hair almost the same red as her tee shirt swinging loosely down her spine. 'The difference here appears to be that you believe you acted correctly, and so I have no justification for my anger. At the same time, you believe I have acted incorrectly, and so you do have the right to your own feelings of anger. Isn't that the way it is, Jonas?' she taunted scathingly.

Jonas drew in a sharp breath, his cheeks pale as he clenched his jaw. 'I wouldn't have put it quite like that—'

'Then how would you have put it?' Her eyes flashed deeply green. 'Please do tell me, Jonas; I'm just longing to know!'

He sighed impatiently. 'There's just no reasoning with you when you're in this mood, Danie—'

'You bet your sweet life there isn't!' she assured him furiously. 'You've set yourself up as judge and jury where I'm concerned—and I have to tell you I find your behaviour arrogant in the extreme. How dare you—?'

Her words were choked in her throat as Jonas moved forward to pull her roughly against him, his mouth coming down possessively on hers, pulling her body in close against his as he demanded a response from her cold lips.

It was a response Danie couldn't give...

She loved this man. It didn't matter that, having learnt what had happened two years ago, he believed the version he had been told without even asking her if it was the truth. She still loved him. And to have him kissing her in this savage, almost contemptuous way, not an ounce of tenderness in his kiss or touch, chilled her in a way that made her tremble.

Jonas pulled away as he felt the shaking of her body, looking down at her with darkened brown eyes. 'Danie...?' he groaned.

She looked up at him with unemotional eyes, only the bruised feeling to her lips telling her this wasn't all a nightmare—one she would wake up from in a minute! 'Let me go, Jonas,' she told him flatly, standing cold and inert within the steel band of his arms.

His arms dropped away from her as if he had been stung; he stepped back, his throat moving convulsively as he swallowed. 'Danie, I—' He broke off as the door suddenly opened behind them, looking sharply over Danie's shoulder at the intruder. 'I thought you had already gone for the day, Dorothy,' he rasped in measured tones.

'I—I had some correspondence to finish,' his assistant muttered awkwardly. 'And as I'm not going straight home this evening—I'll bring these letters back later and put them on your desk—'

'Please don't bother on my account,' Danie told the older woman lightly as she turned to face her, knowing that she had to maintain her dignity until she had at least managed to walk out of here—then she could collapse into the emotional heap of despondency that she really felt she was! 'I was just leaving, anyway.' She smiled brightly at the other woman as she walked to the doorway. 'Thank you once again for everything you're doing for my sister, Jonas.' She made the polite statement without even turning to look at him. 'Goodbye,' she added with a finality that was unmistakable.

Because it was goodbye, if not from Jonas completely, because he was obviously going to continue attending Andie, then certainly from the man she had briefly become emotionally involved with. There could be no future for them now.

If there ever had been.

'I'm terribly sorry, Jonas,' Dorothy told him agitatedly, her expression stricken. 'I had no idea you were in here, let alone that you had company. And I obviously interrupted at completely the wrong time—'

'Stop babbling, Dorothy,' Jonas said wearily as he moved to sit down behind his desk, elbows on its top as he dropped his head into his hands. 'I have a headache.'

'Shall I get you something for it—?'

'It isn't that sort of headache,' Jonas replied heavily, dropping his hands from his face to give her a humourless smile. 'Its name is Danie Summer—and I don't think any sort of pill you might choose to get for me is going to rid me of *her*!'

'I thought she just left,' Dorothy glanced at the open doorway.

'Physically, maybe,' Jonas conceded. He should have just let her leave earlier with her father, not delayed her with that lame excuse of needing to talk to her. Because he hadn't really needed to talk to her at all; he just hadn't been able to bear the thought of her leaving.

'Ah,' Dorothy said knowingly.

Jonas's eyes narrowed. 'Exactly what does that mean?' he grated irritatedly.

'I don't see what your problem is, Jonas.' Dorothy strolled confidently across the width of the office, placing the unsigned letters on his desk for his signature in the morning. 'The two of you were obviously friendly enough a couple of days ago—'

'What makes you think that?' he demanded sharply.

Dorothy shrugged. 'She felt confident enough of your reaction then to telephone you.' She reminded him of the call from Danie she had answered three days ago. 'And you certainly seemed pleased enough to receive the call,' she recalled.

'That wasn't pleasure, Dorothy; I was in a daze. I seem to have been in that state, in one form or another, since the moment I first met Danie Summer!'

Dorothy arched auburn brows. 'And just how long have you known her?'

He thought for a moment. 'Seven days—but it seems much longer!' he admitted, hardly able to believe himself that his acquaintance with Danie had only existed that long.

It seemed as if he had always known her. As if she had always been a part of his life, at first aggravatingly so, and then humorously, followed by a passion that had seemed to consume them both.

And now she had gone. If her final word meant what he thought it did, she had gone for ever.

That ache was back in his chest.

Oh, he knew—being a doctor, he should!—that the emotions didn't actually come from the heart, that it was just another organ of the body—but at this moment he definitely had an ache where he knew his heart to be!

Or, at least, where it should be.

Because he felt as if that particular part of his body had walked out of the room when Danie had...!

'Look, if you've done something stupid, Jonas—and, being a man, you probably have,' Dorothy began, 'then—'

'Not another one.' Jonas sighed his impatience. 'A man hater,' he explained at Dorothy's questioning look.

'Don't be ridiculous, Jonas; I don't hate men,' she chided lightly. 'I just happen to believe women are a little more in touch with their feelings than men, but that doesn't mean I hate men. I doubt your Danie Summer hates men, either. Although, being so beautiful, she's probably had more than her fair share of idiotic men trying to prove how wonderful they are,' she said knowingly. 'Now don't look like that.' Dorothy chuckled at his scowling expression. 'I wasn't referring to you!'

'I should damn well hope not,' he retorted.

'No... Well, to get back to what I was saying,' she continued, a smile playing about her lips at his ongoing bad humour, 'if you've done something to upset Danie then all you have to do is apologise—'

'It isn't as simple as that.' Nothing was ever that simple where Danie was concerned!

No, he was being unfair now. Danie wasn't the one who had complicated things; it was the past that had done that.

Her judge and jury, Danie had accused him of being. Was that what he had been? Had he found her guilty without hearing anything she had to say on the matter?

Possibly, he conceded grimly. But surely those words themselves had confirmed that she was the Danie from Ben's past.

'No one said that life wasn't complicated, Jonas,' Dorothy told him affectionately. 'Maybe it hasn't been for you. You had a happy and carefree childhood—your mother made sure of that. You have a close and caring family. Your career is everything that you could want it to be. You've never really had to fight for anything you wanted. In fact, Jonas—'

'I've had life easy so far,' he finished.

'I wasn't going to put it quite like that,' Dorothy said, 'but in a word—yes!'

'I hope you aren't going to put this little chat down as overtime, Dorothy.' Jonas sat back in his chair, some of the tension Danie's departure had caused starting to leave his body now. 'I'm not going to pay you for insulting me!'

'That's better.' Dorothy looked approvingly at his almost smiling expression. 'And I'm not insulting you, Jonas,' she told him softly. 'I'm trying to help you. Has no one ever told you that the best things in life very often have to be fought for?'

'My mother probably mentioned it when I was younger,' he drawled.

'But so far you've never had to put it into action,' Dorothy guessed. 'Is Danie Summer worth fighting for?'

'Oh, yes!' he answered unhesitatingly, knowing he would never meet another woman like Danie, that there *was* no other woman like Danie. Not for him, anyway. One woman, one man, and he had no doubts that Danie was that woman for him.

But there wasn't only himself and Danie to consider, there was Nikki too. Nikki had just started to find some happiness in her own life. Maybe later on—

Don't be a fool, man, he instantly chastised himself; women like Danie didn't hang around waiting for someone they weren't even sure was theirs.

Because he was Danie's. Heart, body, and soul.

What a mess!

'I really don't understand your problem, Jonas—and I don't want to know,' Dorothy instantly assured him as he raised dark brows. 'But the young lady that just walked out of here looked as if her heart were breaking with each step that she took. It makes no sense if the two of you feel that way about each other.'

'No mountain is too high to climb in the quest for love, is that it?' Jonas derided. He wasn't at all sure if Dorothy had been reading Danie's emotions correctly; if they hadn't been interrupted when they had, angry as Danie had been, she would probably have ended up slapping his face before leaving! 'This particular mountain is just too damned high, Dorothy. And I was never too fond of heights!'

'You don't think an apology would do the trick?' Dorothy ventured.

'What makes you think I'm the one in the wrong?' he demanded.

'I didn't say I did think that—'

'Then why should I be the one to apologise?' Jonas persisted unmercifully.

'It doesn't matter who's to blame for the rift.' His assistant sighed her impatience with his levity. 'Someone has to make the first move, that's all.'

Jonas shook his head, remembering Danie's anger of a few minutes ago, her implacability. 'I'm afraid it won't be me, Dorothy,' he told her quietly.

'Oh, well, I tried,' Dorothy said, glancing at her wristwatch. 'I'm afraid I have to go now, or I'm going to be late; I'm babysitting for Nikki this evening,' she said fondly, having come to know all of Jonas's family during the years she had worked as his assistant.

'She mentioned that,' Jonas replied, feeling a jolt at the mention of his sister so soon after his disastrous confrontation with Danie.

Dorothy nodded happily. 'I'm all for helping the path

of true love run smoothly—and Nikki deserves to be happy after being married to that other swine for so long.'

Without even being aware of it, Dorothy had just answered her own questions concerning why he couldn't chase after Danie. Because he wanted to. He wanted to run after her, tell her that none of the past mattered, that he loved her, wanted her to be his wife. But he always came back to Nikki...

He stood up decisively, following Dorothy through to her adjoining office. 'I think I'll come with you.'

Dorothy paused in the act of pulling on her jacket. 'I don't think it needs two of us to babysit two children,' she commented.

Jonas helped her on with the jacket. 'I didn't mean babysitting,' he replied. 'I'm just ready to leave now too.'

'How cosy—you're going to walk me to my car!' Dorothy teased, moving to switch off the lights.

Jonas took a firm hold of her arm. 'Some lucky man should have snapped you up years ago—it might have helped to curb the bluntness of your tongue!'

'I wouldn't count on it,' Dorothy came back instantly.

Neither would he, Jonas agreed defeatedly.

'I don't think it will have that effect on your Danie, either,' Dorothy continued determinedly as they walked down the corridor together. 'She looks like a woman who speaks her mind, too.'

His mouth was grimly unsmiling. 'Could we just forget about Danie?' he grated.

'I will if you will,' Dorothy rejoined softly.

Meaning that Dorothy knew he wasn't going to do any such thing!

How could he forget the only woman he had ever loved? The *only* woman he would ever love...!

CHAPTER ELEVEN

'WHAT do you mean, my sister is no longer a patient at the clinic?' Danie demanded of the politely smiling receptionist. 'If she isn't here, then where is she?'

Because Andie certainly wasn't back at the estate with their father. Even though it was Saturday, Danie had just come from there after flying Rome up to, and back down again from, the north of England to carry out the business meetings he had cancelled the day before. Andie had been nowhere in sight when Danie had left.

'Miss Summer was discharged late this morning—'

'What do you mean, discharged?' Danie was aware that she sounded a little more than aggressive, but it was just such a shock to have rushed back to town, only to be told that Andie wasn't even here any more.

It had been a long and trying day, most of it spent hanging around waiting for her father to complete his business meetings. It hadn't exactly been a comfortable day either, some sort of tension seeming to have sprung up between Rome and Audrey, meaning that the flights, both ways, had been silent ones.

Danie had had no idea what their problem was, and with her own thoughts on Andie—Jonas she had put into a compartment marked 'private' for the moment; there would be plenty of time to dwell on the agony of loving him in the months ahead!—she hadn't particularly cared, either. But now it seemed that Andie, for all Danie's efforts to get back to town by late afternoon, was no longer here...

'Kay means exactly what she's saying.' Jonas spoke

smoothly as he pushed open the double swing doors to join them in the reception area, obviously having seen her arrival via the security cameras. He was once again dressed in a formal suit, a charcoal-grey one this time, with a steel-grey shirt, and conservatively patterned darker grey tie. 'Andie was discharged this morning and has since left.'

Danie gave him an impatient glance. 'I believe I understood that part,' she said with saccharine-sweetness, her tension high because of her worry about her sister. Besides, it was easier—much easier to her peace of mind—to be angry with this man...!

Jonas looked at her with steady brown eyes. 'Then which part is it you didn't understand? Never mind,' he ploughed on, as she would have snapped a reply, 'come through to my office and we can discuss this more privately.'

Danie didn't wish to discuss anything with him more privately—she just wanted to know where her sister was!

But Jonas stood beside the door he held open for her, waiting for her to precede him down the corridor. With the curious Kay watching and listening, Danie had no choice but to do exactly that, her movements swift in her irritation.

She was dressed very much as she had been the first day they'd met: a black baseball cap hiding her red hair and pulled low over her eyes, a black gilet over a black shirt, and black combat trousers completing the outfit.

If Jonas once again thought she looked distinctly unfeminine—his remarks that day about a short skirt and silky blouse had been duly noted and filed away for future use—then all well and good. She did not want him to see any remnant of the woman he had almost made love with the other evening!

Dorothy looked up to give her a smile as they passed

her office doorway, almost stopping Danie in her tracks as she also gave her a conspiratorial wink.

Now what on earth had that been about?

Obviously Dorothy had realised Danie and Jonas hadn't exactly parted as friends yesterday evening, but even so…!

Danie turned to Jonas as soon as the office door closed behind them. 'Okay, so this is more private.' She repeated his earlier words. 'Now would you mind telling me exactly where Andie is?'

Jonas looked at her impassively. 'You know, you really are one aggressive young lady,' he rasped.

She looked at him unrepentantly. 'The two of us have gone past the need to be falsely polite to each other, Jonas,' she stated. 'Way past,' she added, remembering the things that had been said and done in this office the evening before.

He gave a heavy sigh. 'It doesn't have to be like this between us, Danie. We—'

'There is no "us", Jonas,' she cut in coldly. 'Not any more. If there ever was.'

Jonas seemed to wince at her deliberate coldness. 'Won't you even try to understand—?'

'Oh, but I already do understand, Jonas,' she assured him. 'You know about my past involvement with Ben.' Again he seemed to flinch, but Danie chose to ignore that. 'And you have drawn your own conclusions from that concerning my nature! I don't think there is anything else to understand—is there?'

On closer inspection she had realised that Jonas had a strained look about his eyes and mouth, a darkness beneath his eyes hinting at a lack of sleep. But if the end of their relationship had caused these changes in him—and she wasn't completely convinced of that!—whose fault was that?

Jonas had never bothered to ask her for her version of what had happened two years ago, had simply learnt that she had once known his ex-brother-in-law, and had drawn his own conclusions. He had no idea of the heartache she had suffered once she'd learnt that Ben was a married man, of the agonies she had gone through on Nikki Trainer's behalf, easily able to empathise with the pain and disillusionment the other woman must have felt on learning that her husband had been seeing another woman. Goodness, she still shook with reaction herself whenever she thought of that!

By the same token, Jonas had never questioned the contempt she felt towards men, or the wariness she felt towards relationships. If he had, perhaps he would have realised that the mistake she had made over Ben two years ago was completely responsible for both those feelings!

'There has to be some way, Danie,' Jonas tried, his own remoteness evaporating as he looked at her with longing. 'I thought I could carry on as before, but I—I can't just let you go out of my life!' He paused. 'And you have it all wrong; it isn't your past involvement with Ben that's the problem here—it's my sister! How do you think she's going to feel about my involvement with you—?'

'We don't have an involvement, Jonas—'

'Yes, we do, damn it!' He moved forward to grasp her by her forearms. 'It's okay, I'm not going to try and force the issue in the way I did last night,' he assured her as she looked up at him, startled. 'I realise that was a mistake on my part—'

'Not the least of many!' she snapped up at him.

'Probably,' he conceded, looking at her with pleading eyes. 'Help me a little, Danie!' he groaned. 'I know I've made mistakes where you're concerned, but couldn't you cut me a little slack over that? I've never been in love before!'

Danie stared at him. She couldn't help it. Had Jonas just said he was in love with her...?

No, don't weaken, Danie, she instantly told herself. Anger. That was the emotion she had to maintain here. Because she had no intention of apologising for the rest of her life for a mistake that had come about by Ben Trainer's deceit. A mistake she had already paid for a hundred times over with her own tortured emotions...

She pulled away from him. 'If you think I'm going to just fall into your arms after that declaration, Jonas, then you're mistaken. Words, Jonas,' she derided. 'Just words. Ben used a lot of those too—and look what a liar he turned out to be.'

Jonas's face darkened with anger. 'Don't liken me to Ben Trainer!' he bit out harshly.

An angry Jonas was something to see, Danie noted abstractly, making her aware that, although she had seen him in many moods, she had only once seen him actually angry before this. Those brown eyes were hard as pebbles, his lids narrowed, his mouth drawn into a narrowly tensed line.

Danie expelled a breath. 'Then don't behave like him. He wanted to have his cake and eat it, too,' she stated.

Jonas looked at her hard. 'And in what way am I attempting to do that?' he rasped. 'I'm not a married man—'

'But if I've read you correctly you also want to keep a relationship with me a secret from your sister,' she pointed out, cutting off the description of Ben that made her cringe with embarrassment. 'I may have been naive where Ben was concerned,' she conceded, 'but I don't make the same mistake twice!'

'I'm not suggesting keeping you a secret from my sister, damn it!' Jonas replied furiously.

Danie raised dark brows. 'Then just what are you "suggesting"?' Her sarcasm was only lightly veiled.

He drew in a ragged breath. 'I think I'm asking you to help me find a way to ask you to marry me, while at the same time avoiding making any more waves in my sister's life!' Now his hands were clenched at his sides as he glared across at her.

Marry... Had Jonas really just said he wanted to *marry* her...?

'Don't tell me I've managed to render you speechless, Danie,' Jonas exclaimed. 'That must be a first!'

Danie still stared at him. To be married to Jonas... Wasn't it what she wanted more than anything? But—

There was always a but!

'Jonas,' she began slowly, 'exactly what do you believe happened between Ben and myself?' She looked at him from beneath her cap.

He withdrew slightly. 'It doesn't matter—'

'It mattered a couple of days ago—I saw the accusation in your eyes, Jonas. And no one could mistake the way you've backed off since then.'

He held up defensive hands. 'I was stunned, I admit I was. Oh, not by your relationship with Ben. I was floored by the coincidence of my having met the same Danie. What do you think the chances of that happening actually were, Danie?'

'Without Andie's pregnancy, probably no chance whatsoever,' she admitted, knowing that in normal circumstances their paths would never have crossed, that their lifestyles and circle of friends were completely different. 'Which reminds me,' she remembered. 'You still haven't told me where Andie has gone?'

'Once I had told Andie I was happy for her to go home, aware that you were away with your father all of today, she telephoned your eldest sister Harrie, who came and collected her,' Jonas explained.

So Harrie knew the truth too now, Danie realised. Well, Andie need have no worries, because as a family they would close ranks and protect their youngest member at all costs.

'Don't try and change the subject, Danie,' Jonas grated frustratedly. 'Andie is going to be fine. Your father, as far as I am aware, is in the best of health—'

'I'm aware of that too—now,' she reminded him.

Jonas looked at her searchingly, eyes narrowed. 'Is anger a good option as a defence?' he finally murmured softly.

She raised her head defiantly. 'It works for me!'

'Hmm, that's what I thought,' he said slowly, moving forward so that he stood only inches away from her now, one of his hands moving so that he gently caressed her creamy cheek, his gaze intent on her flushed face.

Danie wanted to step back, away from him, but pride made her hold her position. She wasn't frightened of anyone, let alone—

Heaven!

Jonas's mouth against hers, gently caressing, was absolute heaven...!

If he had been demanding, in the way that he had been the previous evening, then she wouldn't have found it difficult to resist responding, but that gentle sipping and tasting of his lips against hers was her undoing.

Her arms moved up about his neck as she pulled him down to her, not deepening the kiss but drinking him in in the same way he did her...

'Jonas, I— Oops!' came a female voice. 'Dorothy

wasn't in the outer office, and so—I didn't realise I would be interrupting anything.'

Danie had felt Jonas tense at the first sound of the woman's voice, his mouth instantly leaving hers. Although he made no effort to release Danie from his arms.

But even with her back towards the woman, her face slightly buried in Jonas's chest, Danie knew exactly who the other woman was. She might have only spoken to her once, and then only briefly—very briefly!—but that attractive voice wasn't one that Danie was ever likely to forget.

Nikki Trainer.

Ben's wife.

Jonas's sister...!

Somebody up there didn't like him, Jonas decided with an inward groan. A few minutes ago he had asked Danie what the chances had been of her and Nikki ever meeting, now he questioned the chances of his sister walking in on him actually kissing Danie!

Nikki rarely came to his consulting-rooms—none of his family did—and the fact that Nikki had chosen to do so, today of all days, seemed unbelievable to him.

But no, there she was, looking lovely in a peach-coloured silk suit, her face glowingly beautiful as she smiled across the room at him.

Jonas glanced down at Danie, only to find her looking up at him, green eyes dark with distress as she too recognised who his caller was. Of course—the two women had actually met each other on one occasion! Which meant that Nikki would recognise Danie as soon as she saw her face...!

He loved both these women to distraction, and, in the next few minutes, he knew he was going to hurt one of them very badly!

His arm moved possessively about Danie's shoulders as he turned her in the crook of his arm, both of them facing Nikki now as she stood near the doorway. He could feel Danie's tension at the confrontation, his arm tightening about her.

'Well, don't look so embarrassed, you two.' Nikki chuckled as she moved forward. 'Anyone would think you were a couple of naughty children who had been caught doing something you shouldn't!' She reached up to kiss Jonas in greeting before turning to include his companion in the warmth of her smile.

As Nikki came closer, Danie had moved away from Jonas, at the same time adjusting her baseball cap so that it came down low over her eyes, completely hiding her red hair, and putting her face into shadow.

She stood several feet away from them now, but nevertheless Jonas could feel the tension pulsing through her as she tensed for Nikki's recognition.

He drew in a ragged breath, turning back to his sister. 'Nikki—'

'I really should be going now, Jonas,' Danie interrupted, her voice slightly deeper than her normal tone. 'I've taken up enough of your time, and—'

'Please don't leave on my account,' Nikki said laughingly, lightly touching Danie's arm. 'I'm obviously the one who is gatecrashing here. I only called in because I wanted to share some good news with Jonas. I promise I'll be gone in a few minutes.'

Jonas had no idea whether or not Danie had noted the huge diamond solitaire ring twinkling brightly on his sister's left hand, or, even if she had, whether or not she knew of its significance. But Jonas certainly did; his sister's good news appeared to be her engagement to Graham…!

Which was certainly wonderful, and meant that his sister

was about to make a new start in her previously troubled life. But the circumstances for making such as announcement couldn't have been more unsuitable!

'I really do have to go,' Danie insisted, turning to leave. 'I— Thanks for all you did for my sister—er—Mr Noble,' she concluded awkwardly.

Mr Noble! God damn it, he was not going to start all over again where Danie was concerned. Okay, he accepted, as so obviously did Danie, that now was a little awkward, but he certainly was not going back to being called 'Mr Noble' by the woman he loved!

He caught up with her in the doorway, grasping her arm to turn her back to face him. 'I'll be at your apartment at seven o'clock this evening,' he told her.

Danie gave a brief glance in Nikki's direction. 'I don't think that's a good idea,' she muttered.

'Seven o'clock,' he repeated firmly, releasing her arm as she pulled against him; he did not want to bruise the woman he loved.

'If you think it will make any difference.' Danie sighed before striding off down the corridor towards the exit.

Jonas watched her for several seconds, loving her loose-limbed walk, the graceful sway of her hips. He loved everything about Danie—even her damned stubbornness!

'You should have introduced us, Jonas,' Nikki chided as he turned back into the room, his sister now sitting in one of the leather armchairs placed opposite his desk, slender legs crossed neatly at the knee.

He felt in need of a drink after the tension of the last few minutes, but realised that it was only four-thirty in the afternoon. 'Plenty of time for that later,' he dismissed lightly. 'So what's your good news, sis—or do I really need to ask?' He looked down at the glittering diamond ring on her wedding finger.

'Don't try that one on me, Jonas Noble,' Nikki told him reprovingly. 'I just walked into your office, your place of work, and found you kissing a very beautiful woman—and you didn't even introduce her to your baby sister!' She raised blonde brows over teasing blue eyes.

Nikki looked lovely today, glowingly beautiful, obviously extremely happy in her engagement to Graham; Jonas didn't have the right to trample on that. Not today, anyway…

'I don't recall introducing you to any woman I've kissed,' he returned dryly.

Nikki made a face. 'One or two when you were a teenager, but none since then, no,' she conceded.

'There you are, then,' he said with satisfaction, moving to sit behind his desk.

Nikki looked at him with mischievous eyes. 'Surely it's slightly different when the woman you were kissing is Danie Summer…?'

Jonas was glad that he had already sat down—otherwise he might just have fallen down, staring dazedly across the desk at his sister now. Nikki couldn't possibly have recognised Danie, not with that baseball cap hiding her face and hair. So how on earth—?

'Dorothy and I had a little chat last night, Jonas,' Nikki told him conversationally.

'You did what—?' he demanded furiously.

'Oh, do calm down, Jonas,' Nikki told him. 'Dorothy is almost like one of the family. I merely happened to mention to her that you seemed to have a new girlfriend, and—'

'My loyal and discreet personal assistant just happened to "mention" that her name is Danie Summer!' he bit out. 'Damn it, I—'

'Actually,' Nikki cut in, 'what Dorothy said was that you've been like a bear with a sore head this past week—'

'The state of my temper is no concern of either of you,' Jonas barked.

Nikki had known it was Danie beneath that baseball cap all the time! Then why hadn't she *said* something...?

'It is if the reason for that temper has anything to do with me, Jonas,' Nikki informed him softly, totally serious now, that teasing glint having left her eyes. 'Does it?'

He stood up, annoyed beyond words that Dorothy and Nikki had talked about him in this way. 'It did,' he confirmed. 'But I've decided over the last twenty-four hours that I will just have to sit you down and explain the situation to you. Because I intend making Danie my wife.'

Nikki remained calmly composed. 'I'm glad to hear it.'

'It's no good— You're *what*?' He gasped as her last comment finally penetrated his determined thoughts.

'Glad to hear it,' his sister repeated. 'Jonas, I've had months, years, to remember that last meeting I had with Danie. And the thing I remember most about her—apart from the fact that she's very beautiful,' she added, 'is the look of absolute horror on her face when Ben introduced me to her as his wife. She didn't know he was married, Jonas. And she was absolutely horrified at the realisation.' Nikki spoke with certainty. 'And she dumped Ben pretty quickly after that.'

'But the other evening you told Ben—'

'I *taunted* Ben,' his sister corrected. 'I knew damn well he hadn't been involved with Danie Summer after that day I met her at the restaurant. I'm not proud of the fact, but I had a private investigator follow Ben for several months after that day,' she admitted reluctantly. 'How do you think I came by the evidence to divorce him? Which, incidentally, had nothing to do with Danie Summer.'

Jonas had never questioned his sister's divorce, or the reasons for it, knew that the whole subject was a painful one for Nikki. But he had to admit, he was stunned by what Nikki was revealing now...

'You have to believe that I had no idea,' Nikki pleaded, 'when I made that comment to Ben the other evening, that the woman I had dragged you away from was the same Danie Summer. I would never do anything to hurt you, Jonas,' she said huskily. 'Or someone you love.'

He stayed motionless, finding this almost too incredible to take in. All this time he had been frightened of hurting Nikki with his love for Danie, only to learn that he needn't have been concerned after all.

'You do love her, don't you, Jonas?' Nikki prompted gently.

'Do I love her...!' He groaned. 'She's self-willed, out-spoken to the point of rudeness, abrasive, infuriating, ir-ritating, *kissable*—'

'You love her,' Nikki confirmed laughingly. 'And I'm here to tell you not to hold back on my account.' She sobered, looking at him intently. 'I made a mistake when I married Ben, but I have two beautiful children from that marriage, so I'm not going to complain. I certainly don't want you to compound that situation by denying yourself the woman you love out of mistaken loyalty to me!'

Jonas gave a rueful smile. 'I'm afraid that loyalty had already wavered and died. I intended asking Danie to be my wife—was actually in the middle of doing that when you arrived!—and then sorting out the problems it was going to cause within the family later,' he admitted.

Nikki grinned. 'So what's keeping you?'

'Hmm?' he murmured slightly dazedly, stunned to find that all the soul-searching he had done—and no doubt

Danie had done too, once she'd realised who his sister was!—had been completely unnecessary.

Nikki gave him a chiding look. 'You aren't really going to wait until seven o'clock to make that beautiful creature your own, are you? I was listening earlier.'

Jonas shook his head, grimacing. 'You know, I should actually be furious with you and Dorothy for having discussed my private life in this way!'

Nikki laughed. 'Show a woman a single man and she instantly starts matchmaking... We can't help it, Jonas, it's just part of our nature.'

'I'll forgive you this time,' he said. 'Just don't do it again!'

Nikki raised blonde brows. 'Once you and Danie are married there won't be a next time. Mummy is going to be absolutely thrilled,' she said happily as she stood up. 'Two weddings in the family!'

The longing he had to make Danie his wife seemed a possibility now.

If he could persuade Danie to say yes...!

CHAPTER TWELVE

'WHAT kept you?'

Danie came to an abrupt halt, staring at Jonas as he sat in the foyer of her apartment block. It was barely five-thirty, and he was the last person she'd expected to see. He had said seven o'clock, hadn't he...?

After leaving the clinic earlier she had called round to Harrie and Quinn's so that she might reassure herself of Andie's well-being. Her younger sister had been safely ensconced on the sofa in their sitting-room, the usually arrogantly self-assured Quinn fussing over her like a mother hen. A fact Harrie had found highly amusing.

In fact, Danie had still been smiling herself until she'd spotted a relaxed Jonas sitting waiting for her!

She had been stunned by things he'd said to her earlier. Had he really said he wanted to marry her? But he knew how impossible that was—the arrival of his sister Nikki only confirming how impossible!

She looked across at him warily now. 'I've been to see Andie,' she answered slowly.

Jonas stood up, grinning. 'To reassure yourself I wasn't lying concerning her whereabouts?'

Danie gave him an irritated frown as she strode purposefully towards the lift. 'I don't recall your coming into my thinking at all,' she snapped waspishly.

Jonas was laughing softly as he joined her. 'Spoken like the Danie I know—and love.'

She turned to give him one of her looks, relieved when the lift arrived at that moment. 'You said something sim-

ilar to that earlier, Jonas,' she replied. 'It doesn't alter the
fact that I was once involved with your brother-in-law.'
She said this with deliberate hardness.

Didn't he realise that neither of them must ever lose
sight of that fact? Danie felt it more than ever after meeting
Nikki herself earlier. She seemed such a nice woman, obviously adored her only brother; Danie couldn't be instrumental in coming between brother and sister.

Jonas eyed her mockingly as the lift began to ascend
with the two of them inside it. 'Exactly what is your def-
inition of ''involved''?' he drawled.

She gave him another glare. 'Involved is involved,
Jonas,' she stated, determined to remain angry with him;
it was her only defence!

'Did you love him?'

She glared darkly across at Jonas in the confines of the
lift. 'That has nothing to do with—'

'I'm interested, that's all,' Jonas said.

Had she loved Ben? She had been fascinated by him at
the beginning of their relationship, had found his involvement in television interesting, had been attracted to his
dark good looks. But had she been in love with him, even
before she'd learnt of his marriage...?

'No, I didn't love him,' she answered without hesitation,
knowing that it was Jonas she loved—and that she had
never felt anything like this achingly painful emotion before in her life. Certainly not for Ben. He had damaged
her pride more than her heart.

'Good.' Jonas nodded his satisfaction.

Danie eyed him warily again as he added nothing to that
brief statement. Didn't he realise he was just making this
situation worse? There could be no future for the two of
them. At least, not one that would be acceptable to Danie.

She wasn't prepared to be hidden away somewhere so that none of his family should ever know about her.

'I don't see what's good about it,' Danie said as she walked determinedly into her apartment, going straight into the kitchen to put the kettle on for a cup of tea.

'From my point of view it's very good,' Jonas responded, having followed her, sitting down at the pine table as he watched her moving about the room preparing the tea things.

'How did you explain me away to your sister?' Danie was determined he shouldn't lose sight of the obstacles that stood between the two of them ever being together!

He relaxed back in his chair. 'As it happens, I didn't have to.'

Danie's hand shook slightly as she placed the cups on their saucers. Was Nikki so accustomed to seeing unknown women in the arms of her brother that she had stopped even asking? Somehow that explanation did not go down well with Danie at all!

'I'm glad to see you didn't consign my roses to the bin.' Jonas spoke softly.

The yellow roses still stood in a vase in the sitting-room. Not because she hadn't wanted to eliminate every sign of Jonas's presence in her home, but because she simply couldn't wantonly destroy something so beautiful.

'Roses...?' She was deliberately vague. 'Oh, those.' She pretended to remember the golden blooms he had given her on Wednesday evening. 'I haven't been home much in the last couple of days,' she dismissed, placing a cup of tea in front of him, a sugar bowl at its side.

Ridiculous, she thought to herself as she picked up her own cup of tea and sat down opposite him at the table; she loved this man, and yet she didn't even know if he took sugar in his tea!

Jonas smiled across at her. 'This is better service than you gave me on the plane last Saturday!' He ignored the sugar and took a sip of the hot brew.

Well, at least she now knew he didn't take sugar in his tea. Although what good that was to do her, she had no idea; the possibility of them taking tea together again seemed extremely remote!

'I could hardly fly the plane and serve you tea at the same time,' she observed.

Jonas eyed her, amused. 'And here was I thinking you're a woman who can do anything!'

Danie avoided meeting his mocking gaze. 'Within reason,' she muttered.

He reached out and covered one of her hands with his own. 'Danie—'

She pulled her hand away as if she had been burnt. 'Jonas, I have to tell you, having to say goodbye to you twice in one day is not something I'm particularly enjoying,' she said shakily.

'Why not?' he prompted.

She looked across at him with pained eyes. 'I'm just not!' she bit out tautly, so tense now she felt as if her spine might snap. Why did he keep prolonging this? Why didn't he just leave her alone?'

'Does it have to be goodbye?' Jonas said huskily.

Anger flared briefly in her eyes. 'I'm not the sort of woman mistresses are made of, Jonas,' she told him.

'I'm glad to hear it.' He spoke sternly. 'It's not the role in my life I had in mind for you at all—'

Her mouth twisted humourlessly. 'Just as well—*Rome* would probably beat you to a pulp when he found out!' she assured him.

Jonas sat forward, the intensity of his gaze forcing her to look at him. 'That's better,' he said as she reluctantly met his gaze. 'Danie, I love you,' he told her forcefully. 'I love everything about you. And I can't imagine my life now without you in it. Will you marry me?'

She couldn't have turned her eyes away from his now if she had tried. She loved him too. Everything about him. And imagining her own life without him in it was like looking at a barren wasteland. But—

There would always be that but between Jonas and herself…!

Had he misjudged Danie's feelings? She had never said that she loved him. He had told her earlier how he felt about her, but she hadn't reciprocated…

He watched her as she stood up abruptly to move away from the table. The baseball cap still hid the glory of her fiery hair, its peak hiding the expression in her eyes. But he could see her mouth, that delicious, kissable mouth—and he was sure he wasn't mistaken about the slight trembling of her lips before she turned away from him. Unbelievable as it seemed, Danie looked as if she was about to cry!

Jonas stood up slowly, moving to stand in front of her, his hand gentle as he reached out and removed the baseball cap before tilting her face up towards his. He hadn't been mistaken; tears were spilling over her long lashes to fall silkenly down her cheeks.

'Danie…!' he groaned, moved beyond words at this show of emotion. 'Danie, I love you,' he told her as he gathered her in his arms and held her close against him.

'Oh, God, Jonas, I love you too!' she choked, burying her face against his chest as she began to sob in earnest.

Danie loved him! Nothing else mattered. Nothing!

He pulled back to look down at her with eyes that shone brightly with his own love for her, reaching up to smooth the tears from her cheeks. 'Danie, Nikki already knew who you were when she came to my office today,' he told her as Danie's tears came to a halt, and she stared up at him apprehensively. 'Did she look like an angry or avenging woman?' he teased lightly in an effort to reassure Danie.

She swallowed hard. 'Not exactly…' she acknowledged slowly.

'Because she isn't,' Jonas told her happily. 'I have to admit, I've had more than my fair share of uncomfortable moments where you and Ben Trainer are concerned, but—'

'You see,' Danie pulled away from him. 'It doesn't matter if we love each other, Jonas. Your sister will never get over the fact that I made an idiot of myself over her husband. And you'll never be able to forget that I once inadvertently got myself involved with a married man!'

Jonas could easily imagine how angry she would have been once she'd found out Ben was married. He wouldn't like to have been in Ben's shoes during the meeting that followed Danie's discovery!

'When I said I had uncomfortable moments where you and Ben were concerned, Danie, I was referring to my own fear that you might still care for him.' Jonas considered at that moment that it would be less painful to Danie not to tell her about Ben's claim that night at Nikki's house of being able to snap his fingers and Danie would come running. She was likely to do the other man physical harm if she knew about that. Not that Ben didn't deserve it, but Jonas would prefer her to stay out of jail, if possible!

'Don't add insult to injury, Jonas,' she cried. 'I can't stand the man! And I left Ben in no doubt about how I felt about him when I saw him again that evening after I was introduced to Nikki.' She shook her head disgustedly. 'I couldn't believe how I had ever been taken in by him

Jonas gave a sad smile. 'I've come to realise that the last couple of days. So let's just forget about him, hmm?' he encouraged. 'Nikki has,' he added before Danie could make a reply. 'She's moved on, Danie. She's in love with someone else. The two of them intend getting married. In fact,' he continued, 'before I left her earlier I had to dissuade her from suggesting we have a double wedding with her and Graham!'

His sister had thought it a wonderful idea. But Jonas had his own ideas about the wedding he and Danie might have—and it did not involve sharing their big day with another couple.

Danie was staring up at him as if she didn't quite believe him, and he couldn't exactly blame her for feeling the way she did. He had been concerned about Nikki's reaction himself. Although it would have been a reaction, with the realisation of how much he loved Danie, he had been willing to ride out, knowing that he had to have Danie in his life.

At any price.

It was a price he had been willing to pay, although he couldn't say he wasn't relieved it was one that wouldn't be asked of him, after all. That would have been no way for the two of them to begin their life together.

'Danie.' He took a firm grasp of her arms. 'Will you marry me?'

She took a big breath. 'I have one more question to ask before I answer that,' she said. 'Why were you so tired last Saturday at the airport? And how close were you to Grace Cowley?'

Jonas gave a satisfied grin at these signs of her own jealousy where he was concerned. 'That was two ques-
' he rebuked. 'But I'll answer them anyway. I had
most of Friday night bringing a baby girl into the

world. And the closest I've ever been to Grace is as doctor and patient; I'm her obstetrician, Danie. I was in attendance at the birth of her twins!'

Danie moistened her lips, the mere act making Jonas want to kiss her.

'Now answer the question, damn it, woman!' he growled frustratedly, sure that it wasn't usually this difficult to get an answer to a marriage proposal.

Danie continued to look at him searchingly for several long seconds, and then she began to smile. 'I don't think I have anything else planned for three weeks today,' she finally replied.

Now it was Jonas's turn to look perplexed. 'Three weeks today…?' he repeated.

Danie nodded, moving forward to put her arms about his waist. 'If we're going to get married, let's just get it done, hmm?' She arched one teasing brow as she looked up at him.

Danie Summer—soon to be Noble. Beautiful. Infuriating. Soon to be his.

In three weeks, in fact…

EPILOGUE

DANIE gave a happy sigh as she snuggled into Jonas's shoulder. 'I wish everyone could be as happy as we are,' she murmured contentedly.

'Impossible,' Jonas breathed lovingly into her hair.

Danie chuckled huskily, looking around the crowded table, seeing all the people she loved. Her father had insisted that she and Jonas had to celebrate their engagement a week before the wedding itself, inviting all of Jonas's family, as well as her own, to dinner at one of London's leading hotels.

This evening was the result. Danie looked at all the smiling faces: Jonas's mother, his eldest sister and her husband Jack; Nikki with her fiancé Graham; the irrepressible Dorothy; Harrie and Quinn, Andie, Audrey, and finally her father—here she came to an abrupt halt.

Because her father was far from smiling!

'I thought your father approved of our engagement,' Jonas said, obviously having been doing exactly the same as Danie.

'He does,' she confirmed.

'He doesn't look very happy.' Jonas grimaced.

'He and Audrey had some sort of disagreement a couple of weeks ago, and he's been in a foul mood ever since.' Danie shrugged.

'Audrey seems happy enough.' Jonas frowned.

Danie glanced across at her friend and her father's assistant, Audrey laughing at something Quinn had just said to her. 'Yes, she does, doesn't she?' she said. 'Then it's probably nothing serious. Daddy can be a bit too fond of wanting his own way, but Audrey has learnt how to deal with it.'

'I can think of someone else that likes her own way,' Jonas teased.

Danie looked at him. 'Why, who on earth do you mean, Mr Noble?' Her lips twitched as she held back a smile.

Smiling seemed to be something she had done a lot of lately. Not least of all being after her initial meeting with Nikki after she and Jonas had decided to get married. The other woman couldn't have been warmer, or more welcoming to her family, putting Danie completely at her ease after the first few minutes. In fact, the two women had been out shopping together today in search of a wedding outfit for Nikki!

'Oh, I'm not complaining—Mrs Noble-to-be,' Jonas assured her huskily. 'In fact, I'm rather relieved you want us to be married so quickly; I don't think I could wait any longer than next weekend to make love with you!'

It had been a decision they had made together, after Danie had self-consciously admitted to Jonas that she had never had a lover. Their wedding night would be everything it was supposed to be.

Danie was as eager for that night as Jonas was, already sure that their lovemaking was going to be beautiful. After all, how could it be anything else? They were the missing part of each other...!

'I love you, Jonas,' she told him intensely. 'So very, very much.'

'And I love you too, Danie.' His arm tightened about her shoulders. 'So very, very much!'

It was enough.

And it always would be...

HARLEQUIN *Presents* *Passion*™

Looking for stories that **sizzle?**

Wanting a read that has a little extra **spice?**

Harlequin Presents® is thrilled to bring you romances that turn up the **heat!**

Every other month there'll be a
PRESENTS PASSION™
book by one of your favorite authors.

Don't miss
THE ARABIAN MISTRESS
by **Lynne Graham**

On-sale June 2001, Harlequin Presents® #2182

and look out for
THE HOT-BLOODED GROOM
by **Emma Darcy**

On-sale August 2001, Harlequin Presents® #2195

Pick up a **PRESENTS PASSION**™ novel—
where **seduction** is guaranteed!

Available wherever Harlequin books are sold.

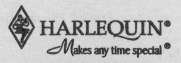

HARLEQUIN®
Makes any time special ®

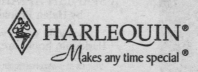

*Harlequin invites you
to walk down the aisle…*

To honor our year long celebration of weddings, we are offering an exciting opportunity for you to own the Harlequin Bride Doll. Handcrafted in fine bisque porcelain, the wedding doll is dressed for her wedding day in a cream satin gown accented by lace trim. She carries an exquisite traditional bridal bouquet and wears a cathedral-length dotted Swiss veil. Embroidered flowers cascade down her lace overskirt to the scalloped hemline; underneath all is a multi-layered crinoline.

Join us in our celebration of weddings by sending away for your own Harlequin Bride Doll. This doll regularly retails for $74.95 U.S./approx. $108.68 CDN. One doll per household. Requests must be received no later than December 31, 2001. Offer good while quantities of gifts last. Please allow 6-8 weeks for delivery. Offer good in the U.S. and Canada only. Become part of this exciting offer!

**Simply complete the order form and mail to:
"A Walk Down the Aisle"**

IN U.S.A
P.O. Box 9057
3010 Walden Ave.
Buffalo, NY 14269-9057

IN CANADA
P.O. Box 622
Fort Erie, Ontario
L2A 5X3

Enclosed are eight (8) proofs of purchase found in the last pages of every specially marked Harlequin series book and $3.75 check or money order (for postage and handling). Please send my Harlequin Bride Doll to:

Name (PLEASE PRINT)

Address   Apt. #

City   State/Prov.   Zip/Postal Code

Account # (if applicable)

HARLEQUIN®
Makes any time special ®

Visit us at www.eHarlequin.com

Coming Next Month